Shards of Faith

His Warriors Book 5

By

Ronna M. Bacon

Verses

Proverb 3:5, 6
Trust in the Lord with all your heart and lean
not unto your own understanding.
In all your ways, acknowledge Him, and He
shall direct your path.

Table of Contents

Chapter 1

*L*ost in the report she was editing, Aideen O'Rouke didn't see the dimming light. She hadn't heard the goodnights from her co-workers. This report had to be done today and it was taking a lot longer than she thought. She raised her head at a whisper of noise, frowning, her short brown hair swinging with the movement, her hazel eyes narrowed. She shook her head. No, she hadn't heard anything. Then the time struck her. She needed to be out of here. She had a dinner to go to in thirty minutes and she had to change. She hurried to shut down her computer, gathering her things and heading for her office door. Then, a louder sound caught her ear and she hesitated, standing close to the wall, straining to hear.

"You sure there's no one else here? There's still a car in the parking lot."

"Yeah, I'm sure. They guaranteed everyone would be gone by 5 p.m. It's six now. He's to be the only one here, so it must be his car."

The harsh whispers sent chills down Aideen's spine. Who was to still be here, her boss? Someone else? And who were these guys anyway?

She cautiously peeked out her door and then crept towards the front door, praying that it would be unlocked. She breathed a sigh of relief when it was. Thrusting it open, she ran for her car, hitting the fob to open the doors. She hit the accelerator, the backend slewing slightly as she raced for the street. She didn't see the man who ran from the building, nor the upraised arm. Shattering glass caused her to jump and scream, to almost lose control of her car. Then she had disappeared from sight.

Where could she go? She was almost afraid to go to her apartment, but she needed to change and then needed to get out of town, literally. Where would she end up?

She stuffed clothing into a duffel bag, grabbed her Bible and her laptop and headed back down the stairs, stopping as she heard voices. It was the men from her office.

How had they found her? She changed directions, running through the hall and down the other steps, shoving the door open hard enough it bounced against the wall. Her breaths coming in gasps, she slowed her steps as she walked away from the apartment. What had she left there that could identify her? Nothing, she thought. She had lived there for three months and had left nothing personal there.

❧❧❧

Samuel Harding stood in the bus depot, searching for who, he didn't know. He had gotten a cryptic message from his father the night before, asking that he meet a client of his coming in by bus. His father hadn't said much more than she was his age, had brown hair, hazel eyes and needed somewhere to stay. Why did his father always send him someone in trouble? The last time his father sent a girl, he had a horrible time convincing her he wasn't her knight in shining armour and that he couldn't stay with her forever.

He turned once more, searching the area, before his dark blue eyes lit on a female, his hand running through his dark blond hair. That had to be her, but still he hesitated, knowing that this time it was different. She was different.

He finally moved forward, his cap in his hand.

"Excuse me. Are you Aideen?" His kept his voice low.

She spun, her eyes round with fright, before he saw her visibly swallow. "And you are?"

"I'm Samuel. Barnabas is my Dad. He told me to watch for a friend."

Her eyes searched the area, then came back to him. "Thank you for meeting me. Mr. Harding said you would have a place I could stay in for a few days."

"I do. Here, let me take your bag." He reached for her duffel, waiting as she hesitated before letting him have it.

Hand to her back, he directed her through the terminal to his car. Opening the door, he waited for her to sit before heading for the trunk and dumping her bag inside. Before heading for his seat, he hesitated, eyes watching her through the back window. Dad, you and I need to have a long talk. You sprung this one on me, now didn't you?

Then his gaze rose. Lord, I have no idea who this is or what she needs, but You do. You've brought her here for a reason. For healing by the looks of it. And I know You're just going to use me again, aren't you?

Samuel turned as he felt eyes on him, searching the area. He couldn't see anyone, but he had felt this before, a long time ago, and that time it had not turned out well. This time, he was determined it would.

He slid behind the wheel and pulled away, his eyes searching the dimming light and then throwing a quick glance at the woman beside him. What was Dad thinking, he wondered, to send her all the way here? Hundreds of miles from where he was at that conference. And why here?

"Where are we going, if I might ask?" Aideen's voice was quiet and tired. She hadn't slept much in the last three days, not with looking over her shoulder for those men and wondering why her contact had sent her this way.

"I have an apartment in my basement I'm taking you to. Dad asked me to hide you away for some reason, and that should do the trick.”

He felt rather than saw the shudder that ran through her. What was going on, he wondered again?

“Yes, that should work. I won’t stay long. I’ll have to leave soon.”

“Why?”

“Why what?” Her eyes turned to him.

“Why would you have to leave soon?”

“I’m a dangerous person to know, it seems, and I have no idea why.”

“Then stay.” He turned into his driveway and parked, turning off the car before facing her. “Stay here and let us help you. We can protect you as well.”

She shook her head. “No one is safe around me.” Her voice trembled as she gripped her hands together, the fingers turning white.

Samuel set her bag down inside the door, and then pointed into the apartment.

“Let me give you a quick tour and explain the alarm system. Here are keys. If you need a vehicle, I have another car in the garage and you're welcome to use it. I just need to add you on the insurance."

She nodded, her eyes taking in the simple floor plan. "There're how many entrances?"

"There are two. There's this one, and then there's one just outside the bedroom. It leads upstairs to my place. It's kept locked whenever someone is down here, but the key is on the ring. I suggest you keep the keys on you at all times."

She nodded once more before turning to him. "Thank you, Mr. Harding."

"Samuel." He watched her turn, flustered.

"I beg your pardon?"

"It's Samuel. We don't use Mr. and Mrs. here in this town much. We're too much a small town."

She nodded, not quite sure she agreed. "Thank you, then, Samuel. If you don't mind, I think I need sleep."

It was his turn to nod. "I left some groceries in the fridge and cupboard for you. Tomorrow, if you like, I can take you to the grocery store and you can get what you want. I work from home, so when you're ready to go, just come around and knock."

Aideen watched him walk away, then stepped to the door, locking it before turning around, her arms wrapped around herself and studying the apartment. She picked up her duffel and headed for the bedroom, liking the colour scheme and the simplicity of the apartment. She peeked into the bathroom, seeing the soaker tub and the stand-alone shower. This was not an apartment, she thought. This is a guest suite. How did God provide this for her on such short notice?

She picked up her purse and dug out her phone, searching through the texts. None from her boss. That worried her. She should have been at work today and he should have sent her a list of what he wanted done. She finally sat on the couch, reaching for the television remote, searching until she found what she wanted. Hand to her mouth, she watched in horror the police presence as her workplace, and then the stretcher with the body bag being removed. He was dead then, she thought, and those men had done the deed. How safe was she?

Samuel sat at his desk, turning his phone over and over, his eyes not seeing what he was staring at. She had gotten to him, he thought, in a way one of their clients hadn't in a long time. He sighed, knowing he had to talk to his father. Punching in the number, he listened as it went to voice mail.

"Dad, it's me. What time do you get in tomorrow? I can't remember if you need a ride or not. Let's plan on dinner if it's early enough."

He hung up, knowing his father wouldn't have answered tonight when he saw it was Samuel. The message he left was in a code his father would understand. He could expect either a voice mail or text message within the next hour. He sat back, eyeing the work on his desk. He needed to work, but his mind was elsewhere that night.

He finally stood, heading for the kitchen where he grabbed a glass of water and downed it, his eyes staring at the calendar, trying to make sense of what had just happened.

Chapter 2

$\mathcal{T}$he tap at the apartment door startled Aideen the next morning enough to cause her to spill the glass of juice she had just picked up. She waited, hand to her throat, as the tap came again. Then, she heard his voice and padded over to the door. She opened the door, stepping aside as she waited for him to enter.

"How are you this morning? Did you sleep well or sleep at all?" Samuel's eyes assessed her, noting the dark circles under her eyes and the paleness of her skin. No, he thought, she didn't get any rest by the looks of it.

"Some." She responded as she made her way back to the counter to wipe up the juice. She turned, glass in hand to watch him, wondering where this was all going.

"Good." He looked down at the keys he had in his hands. "I'm still waiting to

14

hear from Dad and see what he wants to do. I know he's back home. Now, do you need to go anywhere?"

She nodded. "I do. I need some things. I just sort of threw everything I owned into that bag, but forgot to grab my shampoo and stuff from the bathroom. Is there a pharmacy nearby?"

He nodded, as he watched the emotions flickering across her face. Lord, what did Dad and I walk into this time? "There is. When you're ready, we can go. Do you need any groceries?"

She stopped, eyes on the fridge. "I should but I can't."

"Listen, Aideen. Don't worry about the cost. Dad would want you to get what you want and need without worrying about that."

She spun, anger briefly flickering, then dying away as she saw his face. She nodded, then headed for the bedroom for her purse.

Samuel sighed, knowing this would be one of the more difficult cases his father, as an investigator, had gotten involved in.

Samuel had chosen another line of work for himself, but he willingly helped his father when he asked. He knew his father had wanted him to join him in business but had left the decision to him.

"All set?" He waited as she closed the door and locked it before heading for his car. "Listen, I know this isn't what you were planning on, not likely. It never is. Dad's back in town, and we need to sit down with him. I gather somehow you connected with him and he sent you on here. He'll want to find out the rest of why you're running."

"Who says I'm running?" Aideen stared out the window, searching for the men who had chased her.

"You're not? Guess we misread that one, then."

She sighed, finally looking at him, fear in her eyes. "Truthfully? I am. I saw heard something I shouldn't have, and whatever it was about, the men tried to catch me. I think they killed my boss."

Samuel shot her a look, then nodded. "Okay. Now we know what we're dealing with."

"Do you? Really? With just a few sentences, you think you have it figured out?"

"Wow!" Samuel shot to the side of the road and threw the car into park before turning to her. "Listen! I have no idea how you found Dad or he found you. But you two connected. He was concerned enough to send you here. I can tell you it's not the first time he's done this for someone whose life has been threatened. Did you give him your name?" When she refused to respond, he reached and turned her to face him. "Did you give him your name? Answer me." When she nodded, he released her. "Then, with that information, he would have dug up enough facts to know what was going on. He hasn't told me, other than you needed help and a place to stay. I trust Dad to know what he's doing. Now, the question is, can you?" By the time he had finished, Samuel's words had a bite to them.

Aideen finally nodded. "I did give him my name. I couldn't lie to him." Her voice was low enough Samuel had trouble hearing her. She turned, eyes searching the houses near her. "I've brought danger to you. I should leave." Her hand reached for the door handle.

Samuel sighed, then reached to stop her. "No. We need to wait for Dad first. I know he's back in town and is likely finishing up what he had to do. He'll be by today at some point. Look, let's start over. We don't know each other, but it looks as if we're going to be stuck with one another for a while. Let's pretend to be friends, at least when we're out and about. Can you do that?"

She nodded, her eyes still searching the area. "Someone is after me, Samuel. I have no idea why or who. All I know is that my boss is dead." She jumped as her phone rang. She pulled it out and stared at it, her face white.

Samuel reached and gently took it from her hands, reading the text. "Is this from your boss?"

She shook her head. "It's from his phone, but it's not him. He never called me Aideen, it was alway Miss O'Rourke. Who has his phone?"

"We'll find out." Samuel powered it off and then tucked it into his pocket. "I'll drop it off at the police department." He saw the shake of her head and smiled. "Don't worry. I have friends there I trust and can talk to about this without it being official."

She nodded then, her head going back on the headrest. "I don't like feeling like this. I have no family. My friends are going to be frantic looking for me, given what's happened. I need to call them."

"No, that's not a good idea. Whoever it is has likely figured out who your friends are and have people watching them. Are you on social media?"

She shook her head. "No, I'm one of the few of my friends who isn't, but I can imagine they're posting like crazy right now. You're not going to let me check that out, are you?"

He shook his head. "No, Dad won't. Now, let's get your shopping done and head back home. Tell me, you're a secretary, right?"

She nodded. "It's what I do for a living, yes."

"Then I need to hire you. I have so much work backlogged, I'm working fourteen to sixteen hours a day."

"And just what do you do?"

"I'm a title searcher. I've gotten too successful, I guess you could say. I need someone to organize my office. Wait, that won't work. I don't have room in my office to organize anything."

She laughed, and he turned to stare at her. "What's so funny?"

"You are! All of a sudden you've gone from protective to desperate."

He laughed at himself. "Yeah, I guess I did. Listen, if you'd help me while you're here, it would be great. It would give you something to fill your days and you won't even have to leave the property."

He grabbed the bags with her purchases, dropped them on the deck, and grabbing her hand, pulled her to a building just off to the side of the garage. He unlocked the doors, flipping on lights as he entered.

"This was set up to be my office, but I've never used it yet. It's already to go, other than for furniture." He watched as she walked through the rooms, a thoughtful look on her face.

"It's doable." She stopped in front of him. "What about your furniture?"

He nodded, an eager look on his face. "Furniture, yes. We need furniture. Equipment. Phones." He stopped, running his hand through his hair. "Where do I start?"

She laughed again. "I need a pad of paper and a pen to make a list."

"Here, use this." He handed her his phone. "That's the note taking app. List it there. Put down everything you can think of."

She laughed once more. "Are you sure?" She turned as she heard footsteps approaching and stepped back towards what would be Samuel's office.

"Samuel? You here?" A tall man about Samuel's age entered. "I'm sorry. I didn't know you had a guest."

"Andrew! Not a guest, per se, but my new secretary."

"A secretary? Finally getting out of the home office, are you?" Andrew waited for Aideen to speak, his head tilted as he studied her.

"Aideen. Come here. He won't bite, I promise." He reached for her hand, pulling her forward. "Aideen this is Andrew McBeth, a good friend and also the chief of police here in town. Andrew, this is Aideen O'Rourke, a friend who has come to my rescue."

Andrew laughed. "To your rescue, is it now? You need it. Welcome to Elmton, Aideen. It must be your phone Samuel handed me a few hours ago."

Her eyes shot to Samuel, a question in them. He nodded for her to speak. "I guess it would be. Was there anything on it that shouldn't have been?"

"Why would you ask that?" Andrew studied her face once more, seeing the fear lurking there.

"I guess I wasn't sure. My boss was murdered three days ago, I heard the men, and then had to run because they found my apartment. This morning, I got that text purportedly from my boss, only it wasn't."

"And how did you know it wasn't?"

"Because he used my first name. I worked for him for months and all that time it was Miss O'Rourke. That's the way the office ran. We never called one another by our first names, which is bizarre, now isn't it?"

Andrew nodded, his eyes watchful. "What can you tell me about that night? I gather you didn't wait around for the police to show up."

She shook her head, wrapping her arms around herself. "I didn't. I had been working, heard something, realized I was late leaving the office, and gathered up my things. Then I heard two men talking. When I could, I ran for my car and left. Someone shot at me. I managed to get to my apartment and packed. When I was leaving, I heard the two men again. They had found me so quickly. I ran, leaving my car, and headed for a bus station. Then I ended up here."

"You have no idea who they were? No? Then how did they find you so quickly?"

She spun and paced away. "I have no idea. The only way would be if they knew everyone's name and address and realized it was me. That's a possibility, isn't it?"

Andrew nodded, his eyes on his notepad before he tucked it into a pocket. "Let me look into things, on the quiet. I know the chief in that town from conferences. I'll call him and see what I can find out." At her look of fear, he paused. "I won't tell him you're here."

"But if word does get out, I'll have to run again, won't I?"

Andrew shook his head. "No, you won't. Our force here is good. I have friends I can call on. And Samuel there won't let you run. He and his father will look after you."

After Andrew left, Aideen wandered the office, her mind not really on what Samuel had wanted there. She finally turned, finding him watching her. Thrusting his phone at him, she almost ran from the building. Samuel sighed, wondering how far back he had slid in getting her to trust him.

Samuel looked up as a shadow fell across his face. "Dad?"

"Samuel? Finally opening this up as an office?" Barnabas looked around, walking through the building. "I'm glad. It's sat here for so many years. Your mom would be happy."

Samuel blinked away tears at the thought of his mother. "She would be. I hired Aideen as my secretary. It didn't go well with Andrew, though. He dropped by a bit ago."

"Somehow, I didn't suspect it would. He's all cop in situations like this. Is he looking into it?"

Samuel nodded, his eyes on his father. "What can you tell me, Dad, that I need to know?"

"I need to talk to Aideen. Is she around?"

Samuel turned and headed for the door. "She's in the apartment, I suspect. Can you stay for supper?"

"I can. Let me fire up the grill and we'll do some meat." Barnabas studied his son as he walked away from him, almost a mirror image of his father. Lord, I have no idea this time what's up. Usually You give me a few clues, but not this time. You'll have to lead us in this one.

Chapter 3

$\mathcal{A}$ideen watched as Samuel and his father teased each other as they prepared the meal. She had never had that and now realized how much she had wanted that growing up. Someone told her that God would fill the void, but every once in a while she just wanted someone human to interact with.

"Here you go, love." Barnabas set a plate down in front of her. "I hope the chicken is to your liking."

"It looks good. Thank you." She raised her eyes to find Samuel watching her, a look on his face she couldn't read.

Barnabas finally pushed his plate away, wiping his hands on a napkin. "Now, we need to talk, Aideen. I need you to be completely honest with me."

She looked up, fear and surprise on her face. "Completely honest? Do you think I haven't been?"

Hands in the air, Barnabas shook his head. "Not at all. But I need you to go back over what all you saw and felt that night and even before that. Sometimes, it's a little thing that breaks a case."

She nodded, her mind going back to that night, then to the days and weeks before it. Had she seen something or someone she shouldn't have?

"Start with what the business was." Barnabas had risen and retrieve a legal pad of paper and pen.

"It was." Here, Aideen paused, trying to come up for the words she needed. The men waited, not sure where she was heading. "It was an inspection place, for commercial and industrial buildings. I never really go to know what all was involved or who all worked there. Some of the men only came through once a week or so, saying they worked away from the office during the week. I sometimes heard that government officials would be in the building but I never saw them."

"Okay.   So what was your job exactly?"

"I had to read through reports. Checking for details like pricing and material. I didn't really understand it all, but they provided documentation for me to follow." She looked up, horror on her face. "Was the documentation I read bogus?"

"It may well have been.   I've been asked to look into it by someone.   That's how I found you."

She shook her head.   "I don't understand. Why would you be looking for me?"

Barnabas sighed as he fought through what he could and couldn't tell her. Samuel watched his father, then shifted his eyes to Aideen. What had she gotten mixed up in?

"Aideen. Someone asked me to keep an eye out for you. Apparently, they told you months ago that if you needed help, to call me. Is that correct?"

"That was your number?   I had forgotten it until I scrolled through my contacts, trying to find someone I could reach out to. I didn't know." She stood, horror crossing her face. "I've brought trouble to you two now. I need to leave."

Samuel moved to step in front of her. "Sit, Aideen. Sit back down and listen to what Dad is saying. Please? We'll keep you as safe as we can. If I know Dad, he's been asked to keep you here, to keep you safe, to keep you where we can find you if we have questions."

Barnabas nodded as he tapped the chair she had been sitting. "Sit, love. We're not finished, not by a long shot. Samuel, did you have some fresh fruit cut up in the fridge? I think I could use some about now. How about you, Aideen? Can you humour an old man and have some fresh fruit with him?"

Aideen looked up, seeing the twinkle of humour in his eye. She nodded. "If you must twist my arm, I guess I can. Thank you."

Barnabas reached to grasp her hand. "Never run from us, love. Run to us. If anything happens, you get afraid, find Samuel or I. We also have friends you can run to. I hear tell Andrew was around today. Trust him. He and his wife, Phoebe, have quite the story to tell.   We'll have to introduce you to them."

"Not just them, Dad.   How about Josiah and Faith, Mark and Julia, Zeke and Paige, Matthias and Larkin?"

Aideen's eyes grew round.   "Your friends? What happened?"

"They each had what we all call "an adventure".   They went through danger together and somehow managed to fall in love through it all." Samuel smiled at the look of shock on her face. "I'll have to introduce you to them."

Barnabas laughed.   "What an adventure they each had!   Somehow, Samuel, you missed out on getting involved."

"Not totally, Dad." He refused to say that he had been asked to investigate some titles during Andrew's adventure, as they called it.

Barnabas nodded. "Now, back to you, Aideen.   Tell us about yourself, how you ended up working for that company."

She shrugged. "I was put into foster care as a young child. I have no idea who my parents are. For some reason, I never got adopted, never got the good foster homes. I worked various jobs, usually as a temp. That's how I was working there, through a temp agency. I had been there three, four months, maybe? I didn't get to know anyone very well. None of them seemed to know each other well. It was a strange office. A couple of times, I almost asked to be moved to another job, but the pay was good."

"This temp agency? Can you tell me about it?"

She nodded. "It was called Helping Hands Temps. It started up about the time I started looking for work. In fact, I was told I was their first temp worker. They placed me in various offices throughout the city, finally at the inspection place." She looked up, tears sparkling in her eyes. "I wish they hadn't. Maybe I wouldn't have had to run for my life if I hadn't been there."

Barnabas reached out his hand. "We'll never know for sure why God placed you there, Aideen. All I can say is that He is in control, no matter how dark it gets. I'm glad we're able to take you in and give you hope once more."

She snorted, causing both men to stare at her. "Sorry, but God never listened to any of my prayers when I was younger. Why would He listen now? He didn't stop the beatings I had to undergo, the mental abuse, the work I was forced to do at a young age. I never got to be a kid, you see? I never had a childhood. Any foster parent I had worked me and every other foster child they had in their homes. They hid it from the social workers, but we all wanted to escape. I ran a few times but was always found and forced into another home."

Samuel reached out to grasp her hand, his eyes on her face. Aideen watched as his fingers tighten, refusing to look at him.

"That last place, was it really legitimate?" She looked up at Barnabas.

"It seems to be on the surface, but I'm doing some digging. Your boss, now, he's not. I've been mining my contacts in the field. He skirted close to the edge with some of his inspections."

She sighed. "So I was part of it, then?"

"How?" Samuel asked.

"Well, I did prepare the reports for final submission."

"You prepared them on the information you were given. You weren't out there in the field. You didn't have the knowledge to change facts or figures."

She snorted. "And you think that's going to change anyone's mind about my involvement?"

"Now, about this job Samuel offered you? Will you take it and stay here for the foreseeable future?" Barnabas shared a look with Samuel, his eyes narrowing at the look on his son's face. Then, he nodded. Yep, he thought. Samuel's smitten. Lord, help us solve this without them being in danger, at least any more that Aideen already is.

"That job? The one where I have to shop and spend money?" Aideen's teasing took Samuel by surprise.

"That job. We can go tomorrow afternoon. I have to take documents into the courthouse in the morning. You can come with me and see what I do."

She shrugged. "As long as you think it's safe for me to do so."

Barnabas nodded. "For now, it should be. I understand Andrew has your phone. Here's a new one." He reached into his pocket and pulled out a phone, sliding it across the table to her. "No, no protests. Think of it as job-related, okay?"

Aideen finally nodded. "Thank you." She stood and reached for their plates, until Barnabas stopped her.

"We'll do it, love. You go and get some rest. You've not likely slept much in the last few days."

She thanked him and then walked away, their eyes following her.

"Dad?" Samuel's voice was quiet.

"I know, son. She's mixed up in something she shouldn't be, has no knowledge of how dangerous it is, and it's up to us to keep her safe."

Chapter 4

*H*and covering her smile, Aideen watched as Samuel pointed to first one filing cabinet, then another, not quite sure which one he wanted. She finally took pity on him and approached.

"Take the four-drawer lateral one, Samuel." Laughter laced her voice. "Three for the filing room, and then a two-drawer one for your office and my area."

Samuel turned, eyes narrowed, as he assessed her. "You're laughing at me," he accused.

"You're like a little kid in a candy store, not quite sure what to choose."

He stared at her, then laughed as well. "You're so right. I never knew office furniture came in such a wide variety. Now, tell me, is that all the furniture?"

She nodded as she checked her list. "That does it for the furniture. We need to do the supplies and equipment next."

He looked at her in horror. "Supplies? Equipment?"

She patted his arm, having learned to relax around him that morning. "Yes. We need those. If you know of an office supply company, we can do that in quick order. I've done some research and know exactly what I would use, if that's okay with you."

"More than okay," Samuel replied as he tucked his credit card back into his wall. "Thank you. You say you can deliver this all tomorrow? It's all in stock?"

"It is, Samuel." Tom, the store manager, had come out to personally look after Samuel, a friend from high school. "It's going to the office on your property, right? Then, if you're not there, make sure to leave the door unlocked, and we'll get it delivered. Leave a diagram of where you want everything and we'll set it up for you."

"Thanks, Tom. Appreciate it." He held the door for Aideen to leave. "Now, I don't know about you, but I think lunch is in order."

"Lunch? I couldn't do that." Aideen was already shaking her head.

"A business lunch, then, is it? We need to talk over those supplies and equipment you're determined I buy."

Aideen stared at him, then shook her head once again. "You're still like a little kid in a candy store. I'm not sure I should let you loose in an office supply store."

Samuel started laughing as he tucked her into his car and then moved to walk around to his door. He stopped, eyes searching. Something was off, but he wasn't quite sure what. Lord, what's going on? There is no way someone would have found her already, is there? She's hundreds of miles from where she was and traveled by bus. How would they find her?

❧❧❧

Samuel stood in the office doorway two days later, staring around at the changes Aideen had worked with her choices of furniture. He could hear her humming as she worked in the file room. He smiled. He prayed she felt safe with them. He walked quietly across to his office and once more stood, searching the room, before crossing to

38

sit in the chair Aideen had insisted he had to have. He was glad he had gone with her choice of the leather chair. Knowing he would have to be sitting in it a lot, he had wanted comfort but she had found comfort as well as looks. He sighed. He could sit and look all day at his new office, but he really needed to work. He turned to his computer and was soon lost in his work.

Aideen paused for a moment as she heard Samuel crossing the reception area and then went back to placing the handing folders in the drawers and then the file folders in them. She knew they hadn't needed the three cabinets, but Samuel had insisted they get both. Her hands stilling, she thought back to two days ago and smiled as she remembered how excited Samuel had been.

She turned to her desk when she was finished, organizing it the way she liked. The phone rang, startling her enough for her to jerk back. Samuel appeared at the door, his eyes watchful, as she turned to find him.

"I don't know what your company name is, Samuel." Her eyes were wide with apprehension.

"It's Harding Title Searches. Here, let me write that down for you." He turned to look around the area. "I like how you've set everything up. Did we get everything we needed?"

She stared at him, then started laughing. "Samuel, you would have bought out both stores if I had let you. Yes, we have everything we need. The only thing would be some plants in here and your office, if you're willing. There's enough natural light they should do well."

"Plants? Yes, plants. I know just the lady who has them."

She held up her hands. "No, we don't need to get them now. Go back to work, boss, before the clients start complaining."

"Yes, ma'am. I'll just head right back in there." He paused, his eyes searching her face. "Am I allowed to thank my secretary for all her help? Without you, I wouldn't have made the move and still worked so many hours. Having you here will cut those hours drastically, I think." He paused, his eyes on the floor, not quite sure what to say, before he moved back to his office.

At the end of the day, Samuel rose and stretched, feeling like he had accomplished more in that day than he had in a long time. He shut down his computer and walked to the reception area. Aideen had left for the day, and he was disappointed. He wanted to ask how her day had been. He had heard her quiet voice during the day and had only had a few interruptions from her. He liked that she just stepped in and took charge.

Walking back to his home, he looked around. So far, he hadn't had that feeling here that he had had when they were shopping in Oak City. He prayed he never would. He looked up to see his father sitting on his deck, a cup of coffee in front of him, smoke rising lazily from the grill.

"Dad. Hi. Didn't expect to see you today."

Barnabas looked up, an unreadable expression on his face. Samuel sighed.

"You need to talk to Aideen, don't you?"

Barnabas nodded. "She's gone to change. I like how she dresses in her business casual for the office, Samuel. Sets the right tone."

"Is that what it's called? I never knew." Samuel too had liked the slacks and sweater that Aideen had been wearing. "Do I need to give her a raise already?"

Barnabas choked on his mouthful of coffee. "Not yet, boy. Give her a week and then you can. But you'll have a fight on your hands. I left something in the kitchen for you."

Samuel shot him a look and then went to change into jeans and a T-shirt before heading for the kitchen. He stopped as he stared at the small gift-wrapped box sitting on the table. He reached for it and headed for the door, stopping to grab a cup of coffee for himself. Sitting himself by his father, he carefully unwrapped the package, pulling out a desk sign reading "Samuel Harding, Title Searcher" on it. His gaze rose to his father.

Barnabas pointed with his cup. "That's from your Mom and I. She would be proud of you, son, just as I am."

Samuel couldn't see for the sudden tears and couldn't speak for the lump in his throat. He nodded, finally able to speak.

"Thanks, Dad. This means a lot. I just wish she was here to see this."

"Me too, son." Barnabas looked past Samuel to where Aideen stood, not sure if she should approach. "Aideen, come sit. I need to check our meat."

Aideen sat, her eyes on Samuel. "Samuel?" Her voice was quiet.

Samuel rubbed the name plate. "Dad gave me this, from him and Mom. I just wish she was here to see this." He felt rather than saw Aideen rise and move to sit beside him, tears blocking his line of sight. He felt her arms come around him in comfort and he just sat there, letting her.

Barnabas cleared his throat and headed into the house, swiping at the tears on his face. Anna should have been here, Lord, to see this. It's been twenty years since she went home, and I miss her more and more every day. And I know that boy of hers could use one of her hugs right about now.

Barnabas finally pushed his plate away, his eyes focused down the yard. He wasn't quite sure how to broach the subject with Aideen.

"Barnabas, have you any word?" Aideen's soft words cut through the stillness of the dusk.

He turned to study her and nodded. "I do. Let me get you some more tea and us more coffee before I continue."

Samuel watched his father rise and then stood himself, gathering up the remnants of their meals, Aideen helping. They finally settled down in the chairs in the yard, the stars beginning their twinkling in the dark blue of the night sky, the night birds and insects their music.

Barnabas finally spoke. "I've done more research on that company and your boss. So far, I can't find any evidence that they're looking for you here. They seem to still be searching in that town. I can't promise they won't find you, but for now, you're safe.

"Your boss, on the other hand, was a real piece of work. He was being investigated for falsifying inspection reports, at the very least, and more likely taking payoffs. I would say the group of inspectors he had working for him all did the same."

Aideen sat back in horror, thinking of the ramifications of that. "How many people are at risk?"

Barnabas shook his head. "That's what the building department inspectors are trying to find out for sure. It will take months to go back over everything. We suspect he had someone in that department on his payroll." Barnabas paused to take a sip of his coffee.

"Are you sure she's safe, Dad?"

Samuel's voice held a note Barnabas had never heard before. *He's falling for her, isn't he, Lord? Protect them. Protect their hearts.*

"So far we think she is. Unless someone remembers her getting on that bus, and that is always a possibility. She's hard to forget.

"Aideen, that temp agency? As far as I can tell, it was set up with the express purpose of finding you work. You're their only temporary worker."

Her eyes flew to his, shock and then fear in them. "The only worker? Who? Why?"

"I'm working on that one as well. I've had people trace back your foster families and the social workers. We're still gathering information, but it looks as if the social workers were paid to keep you in foster care. I've been told there were couples who wanted to adopt you and before that could happen you were moved to a new area of town or county and your adoption blocked."

"Why?" Tears sparkled in her eyes and Samuel reached for her hand. She gripped his hard.

"That we're still working on. I've found some information on your parents, but need to verify some facts about them before I talk to you. It seems as if the mystery of your birth continues to this very day, Aideen."

She sighed, her head going back and eyes closing. "Why? Why did it have to be me?" She stared at Barnabas. "How safe am I really?"

"I see no immediate danger."

"Then why do I feel like I'm being watched, that someone is out there."

Barnabas shared a look with Samuel who nodded.

"I've felt it since the night I found Aideen at the bus terminal."

"And you never said anything?"

"Sorry, Dad.   It wasn't anything definite, just a vague feeling."

Barnabas sighed.   "I know those feelings too well, Samuel. Keep your eyes open, okay?"

Samuel nodded, then rose as Aideen stood.   "Heading for your rest, Aideen? Sleep well."

Samuel sat back down, his eyes on his father. "Where do we go from here, Dad?"

Barnabas shrugged. "I'm still working on some stuff. Has Andrew been in touch?"

Samuel shook his head.   "No, he hasn't. I didn't expect him to yet."

Chapter 5

The man shifted in his seat, his heavy body not comfortable in his car, his eyes on Samuel's house. He had found her, just by chance. Now, he would watch, waiting for the proper time to grab her. His phone out, he made his call and got his instructions. His eyes followed Aideen as she walked towards the office building, then entered it. Yes, it was her. Waiting wasn't something he did well, but this time he would have to.

Aideen looked around the office, trying to decide what more was needed. She sighed, wishing this was really an office she would work in for years. She enjoyed what she had done so far. Samuel was an easy-going boss. She smiled. Not a boss at all, she thought. He didn't have a clue how to be one.

She looked up as Samuel entered, piles of folders in his hands.

"What is all that?"

He looked sheepish. "I found these this morning. Can you go through them, make sure there's nothing there I should have filed?" He ran his hand through his hair. "I just feel like I've been so far behind all this time."

"And now I think, other than this, we have you caught up. You have two calls to make right now, regarding that one property. I've left the numbers on your desk. If I have any questions about these, I'll come and ask."

Samuel nodded, his mind already on the calls he was making that day and the research he had to do. He sighed. It just never stopped. He pulled his phone from his pocket as it rang. Bill Buckley! Now what would the detective friend of his be wanting?

"Bill. How are you? What can I do for you?"

Bill's voice had a touch of humour as he spoke. "I hear you've finally set up your office. Listen, I need some research done on a property for me."

"What's the address and how soon?" Samuel nodded as he jotted down the information. "Okay. Let me have a couple of days. I'm deep into something right now, but should be able to get to this tomorrow. Okay. Talk to you soon."

He looked up later that day as Aideen tapped as his door and then entered.

"Here's what I found, Samuel. These need to get to the town hall today. You still have time to do that. These pile you need to look at by Monday."

He sat back, eyes on the paperwork she had sorted and prepared for him. "Are you sure you haven't done this before?"

She shook her head, a smile on her face. "No, I haven't, but it's not hard. Just a matter of learning the ropes and the timelines. That kind of stuff I've never had an issue with."

"Okay. So this has to go to the town? Come with me. I'm going to introduce you to the clerks I deal with. In future, if everything's all ready to do and I've signed off on it, you should be able to do it. Oh. I do need your license number to add to the insurance on the other car."

"I've taken care of that for you."

He looked up. "You have?" At her nod, he stood. "Well, then. Let me find you a set of keys and you'll be good to do. You did tell them it was the business car?"

She laughed. "They knew that. Your town is small. I guess it's true what people say about small towns."

"What's that?"

"Everyone knows your name and your business."

He laughed. "I guess they do. I was born and raised in this town. Everyone looks out for the other."

She shook her head again. "I'm not used to that." She stopped, her eyes going to the car sitting at the curb. "Do you know whose car that it?"

"It's not one I know. Why?"

"It's been sitting there all day and someone has been in it."

Samuel stopped her from opening the office door, pulling out his phone. "Bill? Samuel. Can you track a plate for me? The car has been sitting out in front of my place all day, Aideen says. Here's the description and the plate number."

He drew Aideen back to one of the chairs and pushed her down, before going to the office phone.

"Tracy, Samuel. Look. I have some paperwork that needs to be filed today and I'm stuck here at the office. Great. Thanks. Appreciate that."

Ten minutes later, Aideen looked up to see an older woman stroll through the door.

"Tracy, thanks for coming. Here's the folder with it all. Aideen, my new secretary, has organized it all for you."

Tracy flipped through the paperwork and smiled. "This is wonderful, Samuel. It will be filed tonight." She turned to Aideen. "And thank you.   Samuel's one of our favourites at town hall.   He always has everything ready, but the way you've organized it makes it so much easier. Welcome to town."   With that, Tracy breezed back out the door.

Aideen sat, staring after her with her mouth open, snapping it closed when Samuel laughed. She glared at him.

"That's Tracy from the town hall. I usually deal with her. Now you can. And, yes, she's always been a whirlwind." He turned to pace to the window. The car had gone. "Whoever it was is gone. Let's head for the house while he's not out there."

Aideen stood, legs shaking as she walked towards the door. Samuel caught her hand, giving her some stability as she moved towards the house.

"This is Thursday, Aideen. Dad and I usually head for the Bible study at our church. You're welcome to join us." He watched as she shook her head, his heart dropping just a bit.

"I think I'll just stay in, if you don't mind. All this has drained me."

❧❧❧❧

Aideen shifted restlessly on her couch, not having made it as far as her bed that evening. She lay half-asleep, not focusing on anything, when she heard the scratching at her back door. She rose, heart in her mouth, feeling for her keys. She moved silently to the door to Samuel's apartment, finding the key, slipping through the door and locking it again, rushing up the stairs as quietly as she could.   She searched for somewhere to hide, somewhere no one would find her.   Not finding a place, she stood, eyes searching into the darkness, hearing the knob shake on the door she had just came through. Then she heard nothing! Silence met her ears.   She tiptoed to the back, watching as the dark shape hesitated at the deck stairs, and then disappeared as lights came from the driveway.

Samuel flicked on the light, blinking as he saw Aideen standing there. Barnabas stood behind him, then disappeared. Samuel moved towards her as she backed away.

"Aideen? What happened?"

"Someone tried to get into my apartment. I came up here, like you told me to.   When they say your lights they disappeared. I think they knew I had come up here." She spun, walking away from him into the living room.   "What did I do, Samuel? How much danger did I bring with me?"

Samuel stood for a moment, then came up behind her, his hands on her shoulders. "You have done nothing. You were right to come up here."

She turned, eyes shadowed as she searched his face. "I need to leave. I've brought trouble to you and your Dad."

"Not happening, Aideen." Samuel looked back at his father. "Come here. Sit. Let me get you some tea, okay? Then, we'll talk."

Samuel moved quietly around his kitchen, his eyes bouncing between Aideen and his father. When he had given her the tea, his father nodded towards the outside. Samuel watched Aideen for a moment, then moved to the deck.

"What did you find, Dad?"

Barnabas blew out a breath. "Someone picked her lock, I can tell. I didn't go in. I left that for the patrol officers. Someone should be here soon." He nodded towards the kitchen. "Did she say anything?"

Samuel shook his head. "Other than someone broke in and she made it up the stairs. I don't like this, Dad. How did they find her?"

"The plate you had Bill run? It belongs to an investigator. That's likely how." He turned in a circle, searching the area. "Now that they know where she is, we'll have to take more precautions."

Samuel nodded. "She's already feeling guilty." He headed back for the door. "Let me know what the officer says and what we can do to up the security for her."

Aideen watched as the patrol officer pocketed his notebook and stood to leave. Barnabas followed him as Samuel turned to study her.

"Aideen?" Samuel had to call her twice to get her attention. "What are you thinking?"

"I'm thinking I should just get back on that bus and keep going." She sighed, her head dropping to her folded arms.

"Not happening. Dad's working on something, says he wants to talk to you sometime tomorrow."

She looked up with bleary eyes. "Today, you mean." She stood, heading for the door. "I'll see you in the morning, Samuel." She was gone before he could stop her.

Barnabas stood and watched her, then moved to the driveway, his eyes searching. No one was there now, but they certainly knew where she was. He would have to work hard to protect her. He turned to return to the house, stopping as something white caught his eye. He bent, picking up the envelope laying there.

Samuel watched as his father carefully laid the note on the table, not quite sure what was going on.

"Samuel, it's worse than we thought."

"What do you mean, Dad?" Samuel moved to read the letter.

"It seems they know where she is and are looking for information they think she has."

Samuel snorted. "She has nothing. She also says she doesn't remember what was in the reports, she had had to review so many." He paused, reading the note again. "We have to tell her, don't we?"

"We do. Pray she doesn't pick up and leave."

Samuel sighed. "She's already threatened that, Dad. Now what?"

"Now what is that we get some sleep. Turn in, son. I'll take the couch."

Chapter 6

"Samuel?" Aideen stood in his office doorway the next afternoon. "It's Friday afternoon. You told me to remind you that you had plans for tonight."

Samuel's head raised and he blinked to focus on Aideen. "I do. What time is it?"

"It's 4:30. Now, you need to get up from that desk and go on with your plans. I know what you're working on can wait until Monday."

"It can." He rose, tided up the papers and then walked towards her. "I'm having dinner with some friends. You're welcome to join us."

She stared at him, then shook her head. "Thanks but I think I'll have an early night. Your Dad said he'd be by in about an hour to talk with me."

"He did?"   Samuel looked torn, wanting to keep his commitment to his friends, but not wanting to leave her.

"Go, Samuel. I'll be fine. Your Dad put a new lock on that can't be picked he tells me."

Samuel laughed as he set the alarm and then locked the door behind them. "That he did. So tell me, how was your first week?"

"I've enjoyed it. It's all strange and new but it's interesting."

Samuel nodded, his eyes straying to the street. Bill hadn't gotten back to him yet with the results of the note and he didn't like that.

"Stay safe, tonight. Make sure your doors are locked. Go upstairs if you need to." He paused at the deck stairs, then shook his head.

"You were going to say something?" Aideen watched him.

"I was, but it can wait. Have a good evening."   He watched as she closed the door behind her before heading for his own door, a thoughtful look on his face.

Zeke watched Samuel as he stood and talked with Matthias before walking towards them. The only friend missing tonight was Noah, who had promised to be there and then had to cancel. He shook his head. Noah just didn't seem to be around much.

Samuel turned, lost in thought for a moment. Zeke studied him for a moment, a frown in place.

"Samuel? You're not here, buddy. Where are you?"

Samuel looked up, eyes watchful. "No, I wasn't. Just thinking about something."

Zeke nodded, not prying. "How's the new office working out?"

"Great. I wish I had moved out there months ago. It's nice having the separation between home and office."

"And your new secretary?"

"She's picked everything up quickly, thank goodness. My office is well organized, my filings are ready to go ahead of time, and I can do what I love."

"Sounds good. But what do you really know about her?"

Samuel stared at Zeke and caught movement from Jonah, another friend, who stood nearby. "Dad's the one who sent her to me. She's on the run from something bad and is scared stiff at times." He sighed. "I just don't know what all it is, though. Dad's working on the investigation but hasn't said much."

Jonah and Zeke shared a look and then a nod.

"Your Dad's not saying much?" Jonah questioned.

"No, he's not. It's not unusual for him to be like that. Thing of it is, she had someone break into her apartment last night."

"Her apartment?" Zeke asked.

Samuel nodded. "Dad and I were at Bible study. The patrol officer wasn't too helpful in finding much. There was also a car hanging around yesterday that I had Bill run the plates on. Dad recognized the name as an investigator from Oak City."

"How did they find her?" Jonah shook his head. "You said she came in by bus?'

"She did. Unfortunately, she's the type of person you see and don't forget." Samuel turned as his name was called and he walked away

"He sounds like you and Paige, Zeke?"

Zeke grinned as he nodded. "I noticed that too. How can we arrange to meet this lady?"

Jonah shrugged. "I have a feeling they're keeping her under tight wraps, as least Barnabas is. He doesn't place someone in that apartment lightly."

"No, he doesn't"

ʘʘʘ

Aideen hesitated as she heard the knock at the door, waiting until she heard Barnabas' voice, before unlocking it.

"And how are you tonight, Aideen?" Barnabas' keen eyes assessed her.

"Tired, as you well can expect. You wanted to talk to me?"

"Let's sit. I have some things to discuss with you and show you."

Aideen nodded. "Then we need coffee, I take it?" She set a mug in front of him.

"Aideen, before I sent you here, I prayed long and hard. I knew I would be involving my boy in something he's never been involved in before. The odd time, I have asked him to provide transportation and sometimes a couple of days longer of help. It's not something I do lightly. This time, it was different." He paused, his eyes on his folded hands. "I knew it would be different for him and you." He raised his eyes to her face. "When I heard about what you were going through, I thought of how I would want my own daughter treated if I had had a girl. That's why you're here."

She nodded. "I've told you I've never had that, Barnabas. Never had a home. Never felt loved. Here I do. I know you care."

He nodded, then looked down at the folder he had set on the table. "What I am about to tell you will explain why I wanted to help you. You can tell no one, not even

Samuel. Not at this point. It has become extremely dangerous for you. If I could find somewhere to hide you away, I would. I don't like leaving you here in the open and at risk. And I certainly do not like putting my only son at risk."

"How bad is it?" Aideen sat back, a scared look on her face.

"You said you were raised in foster care and that no one wanted to adopt you. That is far from the truth. I need to go back to your biological parents. Strange as it may seem, I knew your parents. I was at college with them before we graduated. Your father was brilliant. He started up a company that had cutting edge technology in my field. I can't give you specifics as they are confidential, but I can say it has made a huge difference in how we operate. Your parents were out for dinner one night, about three months after you were born. They and four others were killed in a drive-by shooting blamed on a gang, but investigators have always felt that they were the real targets, likely from a competing company. You were put into foster care and disappeared into the system before any of their relatives could get to you. In fact, it was the night they were killed.

"Your family relatives tried for years to find you, with no success. Unfortunately for you, they have all passed on. Now, regarding the adoption. There were at least six adoption applications put forward for you, but for some reason, they were all rejected. I'm working on finding out why. You were always placed with foster parents who were, to put it nicely, shady, ready to hide your for the right amount of money." He looked up at Aideen as he said this.

She nodded. "I knew they were bad, but I didn't realize how bad."

Barnabas continued. "When you graduated from high school, you were directed to that temp agency. As I said before, you were their only worker. They placed you in those companies because there was material there they wanted to get out of the company. They used your paperwork to cover this. You weren't supposed to be there that Friday night. You were supposed to have been gone by the time the men arrived."

She shuddered. "So it was planned all along?"

He nodded. "It was. Unfortunately, we can't prove that right now. The man who broke into your apartment last night was the one who was sitting out front watching you. Bill caught him. He's not saying a thing."

She drew a deep breath. "I see. Now what, Barnabas? I like this town. I like my work. Do I have to leave?"

Barnabas shook his head. "Not at all. We're working on something to keep you safe. Samuel as well."

"Samuel!" She stood and paced. "I can't be near him. He's at too much risk."

Barnabas smiled. "Not at all, Aideen. I'll talk to him in a few days. What we need to do is to come up with a plan that if you are approached, you have options to follow."

She sat back down, a huge sigh quivering through her. "Okay. Let's plan. I can't say that I like this all that much though."

Barnabas laughed. "That's the spirit. That's what keeps you alert and alive."

"I certainly hope so. Why are you really doing this, Barnabas? It's not just because you were friends with my parents."

He stared at her, trying to made a decision, and finally spoke. "It is, Aideen. Your father was like a brother to me. We agreed that if something happened to one of us, we'd watch out for the other's family. You disappeared before I could do that. When a contact approached me with your name last week, I had to help you."

"You need to tell Samuel all this. That's the only way I'll consent to this. I can't hide anything from him. He seems to be able to read me too well already."

Barnabas smiled. "He does, Aideen."

His heart cried out for protection for these two young people. Lord, Aideen is struggling with her faith. She needs that renewal to come on her. Lead her that way.

Chapter 7

Samuel turned as his father approached him the next morning, a thoughtful look on his face.

"Morning, Dad. You're late!"

Barnabas shook his head as he laughed. "That I am. I had a call come in early this morning that took longer than I expected. How was your dinner last night?"

"It was great." Samuel slid a plate of pancakes in front of his father. "Seems strange though with half our group married."

"It would. You eight men have been friends now for what, ten, twelve years, if not longer?"

Samuel nodded. "We have been. Do you know what's going on with Noah? He's not been around much lately and we don't hear from him much."

"Can't say that I do. I talk to Seth once in a while, but even he doesn't have much knowledge of what's going on. These pancakes taste just like your Mom's."

"Thanks, Dad. I was hoping they did." Samuel laid his knife and fork on his plate. "Now, something tells me you wanted to talk to me other than just catching up on last night. You sounded serious when you called yesterday afternoon."

Barnabas took a sip of coffee to delay his response. He sighed. "It is, son. I talked to Aideen last night. I've tried to keep you out of all of it, but she insisted you needed to know what was going on."

"And what exactly is going on? You've been keeping something back, I know." Samuel's eyes stayed steady on his father.

"I have and I would have preferred to keep it that way." He paused, gathering his thoughts, and then proceeded to tell him what he had told Aideen the day before.

Samuel stared at his father. "You knew her parents?" At his father's nod, he continued, "Then why didn't you tell us that before?"

"It's like this, son. I had to verify facts and I'm still working on that. Bill and Andrew are aware of what's happened in the past. Bill, in particular, is working on his own time to help. We need to keep Aideen safe. Whoever set up this elaborate ploy so many years ago is still out there. What I have determined is that because no one could prove that Aideen was in fact dead, the monies from her parents are sitting in a back account. She's a wealthy young lady, Samuel. She has less than a year to come forward or it goes to charity. What I have been told is that people are trying to declare her dead in order for it to go to her next of kin."

"But I thought you said they were all gone."

"They are. That's what I can't figure out, who they think the next of kin is."

Samuel sat back. "Who would it go to if she married?"

Barnabas nodded. Samuel had gone right to the centre of it. "If she's married and dies, no matter her age, it goes to her husband."

"So we can expect someone to come forward and claim to be her husband."

"That's what I'm expecting to have happen. How do we prevent that? I'm working on a plan. And it involves a number of steps and people."

"Keep us informed this time, will you?" Samuel stood and gathered their dishes. "Does Aideen know this last bit?"

Barnabas shook his head. "That was the call I got this morning, confirming this. I'll need to talk to her today."

"She's gone out. I talked to her before you came and gave her this week's pay. I certainly had a fight on my hands over that."

"What, too little?" Barnabas grinned at the glare he got from his son.

"No. She insisted she didn't need that much, that she had a home here she needed to pay for. I finally convinced her that what she received with average for her work."

"And now try to raise her pay."

Samuel laughed. "Yeah, I can see that will be easy to do." He turned, leaning against the counter. "Listen, Dad. How is her faith?"

"That I can't get a handle on, son. I know she believes from what she's said, but she doesn't have that deep down faith that will get her through this."

Samuel nodded. "That's the impression I got to. Now I know how to pray for her."

❦❦❦❦

Startled, Aideen looked up when she heard her name called. Her hand stilled on the rack of sweaters she was looking through, fear seeping through her. Then she relaxed.

"Tracy! How nice."

"Aideen! I was hoping to find you out and about. Do you have time for a coffee or do you have something else to do?"

"I was just browsing. I need to get some more clothes, the ones I have are old."

"Well, let's find you some clothes, and then we'll do coffee."

Aideen watched in amusement as Tracy took over, finding her bargains she hadn't planned on. Then, feeling eyes on her, she looked around. No one stood out, but she knew someone was there.

73

"Aideen?" Tracy's voice brought her attention back to the woman standing beside her.

"Sorry, Tracy. I got lost there. Is this it then?"

"If you insist, it is. Come on. There's a nice little coffee shop just down the street. Drop your stuff in your car and come with me."

Hours later, Aideen folded the last of the clothes she had found and then headed for the back yard. She needed to get outside for a while. Walking slowly around, she stared at the gardens. They really needed work to clean them up.

Samuel found her on her knees, hands into the dirt. He stopped, his hands full of grocery bags and watched her in silence. He liked that, he thought. She suited his backyard. Then he shook his head. No, that wouldn't work, not at all.

ﻷﻷﻷ

The next morning, Samuel tapped at Aideen's door, waiting until she answered before grinning at her.

"Morning, Aideen.   Thanks for working in the gardens."

"You're welcome."   Aideen was surprised at his thanks. "I enjoyed it. But that's not why you're here."

"No, it's not. I was wondering if you wanted to come to church with us this morning."   He was hesitant to ask, not wanting to push.

She stopped for a moment, her head already shaking a refusal. Then, her eyes searched his and she nodded. "I can. I just need to change."

"What you have on is fine. We're not fancy dressers there. At times, you'll find our pastor in jeans on a Sunday morning."

Samuel watched as Aideen searched the sanctuary, her eyes constantly moving, her nervousness showing in her tenseness. He finally reached and touched her hand. Startled, she looked up at him and then at Barnabas sitting on her other side.

"You're fine here, Aideen.   It's not likely what you're used to."

She shook her head.   "No, it's not. Any church I ever went to was so formal.

You can't say that about this." She looked up as she felt eyes on her. A couple stood at the end of their row, greeting Barnabas.

"Aideen, these are my friends Zeke and Paige. This is Aideen."

Before she could speak, the service had started. She turned to the front, a puzzled look on her face. This wasn't what she was used to, not at all. She watched the congregation and turned her attention to Samuel.

He smiled and leaned over. "Not quite sure about us? We alternate between old hymns and modern worship music every other week."

She nodded, her eyes on the words on the screen at the front. A sudden longing came over her, to know the peace that Samuel and Barnabas had, but she wasn't sure how to go about getting it.

❧❧❧

Later that week, Aideen stood from her desk and walked through the office. She had been here for almost two weeks and was just starting to relax, to feel safe. But there was something worrying her, something she couldn't quite remember and it had to do with her old boss. She turned as the office door open and she hear heavy footsteps. She waited, then heard the footsteps heading her way. She fled to the back door, opening it quietly and then making her way to the garage, where she hid. Who was it? She knew it wasn't someone who should have been there. They hadn't spoken.

Samuel headed for the office, his eyes studying the car parked at the road. He wasn't expecting anyone in for an appointment and his wasn't the type of business to encourage drop-ins. He stopped just inside the office door, eyeing the two men who stood there.

"Can I help you with something?"

The taller of the men turned. "Yeah, you can. My sister's supposed to work for you. We dropped by to say hi."

"Your sister?   You must have the wrong office." Samuel stood to the side of the open door and pointed. "I think you need to leave."

The second man slammed the door shut and shoved Samuel against the wall, his arm across his neck.

"Yeah, my sister. I know she works here. I've seen her around here. Now, where is she?"

Samuel shook his head as best he could. "No one here fits that description. Now leave."

Samuel crumpled to the floor from the blows directed at him. Through blurry eyes, he saw the two men search the office once more and then walk away without a backwards glance. His eyes slid shut as blackness threatened him. How much later, he didn't know, he felt soft hands on his face and a frightened voice calling his name. He groaned as he moved, darkness settling in once more.

Barnabas stood, arm around Aideen, as he watched the paramedics work over Samuel, his eyes worried, face stoic. He could feel the shuddering breaths she was drawing, but his attention was on his son.

"How bad is he, Ezra?" Barnabas' voice was rough.

Ezra spun around to study Barnabas. "Lots of bruising coming up, Barnabas. We'll have to see what the physician says." He turned back to his assessment, quiet words spoken to his partner and then to Samuel.

Samuel drew his right leg up as Ezra touched his abdomen and groaned. "Yeah, right there, Ezra. You don't have to poke it, you know."

Ezra gave a half smile, then turned his attention back to his partner. They had worked enough together to know what the other was thinking.

"Samuel, we're going to move you to the stretcher and then off to Emerge."

"Ezra, I don't need a play by play of what you're planning. Let's just do it, okay?" Samuel's voice was tight with pain. As they lifted him, his eyes closed, and he drifted off into blackness again.

"You riding with us, Barnabas?" Ezra turned to him on the way by.

"No. I'll drive and bring Aideen with me. We'll meet you there." He turned as Bill stopped beside him.

"Barnabas?" Bill's voice held a question and a statement.

"We don't know what happened yet, Bill. Aideen found him. Apparently she hid from the two men earlier and Samuel must have walked in on them." He looked down at Aideen, whose eyes were following Samuel. "The patrol officer took her statement."

Bill nodded. "I got the gist of it from him. Why go after Samuel?"

"Likely because they couldn't find Aideen. She did good. She ran to the garage and hid, just where we showed her."

Bill stared at him. "And just why would you have shown her that?"

Barnabas sighed. "It's a long story, Bill, and I can't give you all the details. Not yet, anyway." He was more worried than he let on. "Suffice it to say, someone is after Aideen, has been all her life, and likely set her up to take the fall for her boss' murder, or that's the scuttlebutt I'm hearing."

"We need to talk." Bill was angry and let it show.

"We will. Right now, thought, I'm heading after my son. Find me there." Barnabas pointed the way the ambulance had gone, then led Aideen to his car, shutting the door after her, and staring around. They were there, he knew, there and watching everything that went on. Somehow, they had found her.

Barnabas paced the floor of the waiting room, his mind racing, his eyes watchful. He turned to study Aideen, who sat, head down, arms wrapped around herself, quiet. He finally sighed and sat beside her.

"It's not your fault, Aideen."

She raised her head, her eyes bleak. "It is, Barnabas. If I hadn't come here, Samuel would not have been beaten up. I need to leave."

Barnabas' hand on her arm anchored her to her chair. "Let's get one thing straight. This is not your fault. It's whoever behind this that is responsible. Both Samuel and I knew what we were walking into when we agreed to help you."

The doors swishing closed behind him, Bill stood for a moment watching Aideen, before shaking his head and moving to sit beside her.

"What do you go and get yourself involved in this time, Barnabas?" His question was quiet but loaded.

"Still working that one out, Bill. I haven't talked to Samuel yet to find out what actually happened. Until I do, I can't tell you."

"Aideen?"

She started as Bill spoke her name, then shook her head. "You have my statement. I don't know anything else."

"Be that as it may, a friend is in Emergency because of you."

Aideen stood, glaring at Bill. "You know what? No one has to take this from you, police officer or not." She spun and walked rapidly away from them.

Barnabas was on his feet. "I would rethink your questioning tactics with Aideen, Bill. If I have to, I'll talk to Andrew and have you removed. She's been through more than you can ever imagine throughout her whole life. She's not the criminal."

"Are you sure?" Bill stood, almost toe to toe with Barnabas, not backing down.

"We're done with this conversation, Bill. I'll be speaking with Andrew." Barnabas followed Aideen, who had stopped to speak with the ward clerk.

"He's right, Bill. You do need to approach this differently." Andrew stopped beside Bill. "I've talked with him about Aideen."

Bill blew out a breath of frustration. "I know I should." He watched as the two moved back into the examining room area. "Now what?"

"Now what? First, you'll apologize to them both and to Samuel. Then we move on in the investigation. Barnabas was by earlier today. He left what he could of his own investigation. This goes a lot deeper than even I thought."

Bill stared at his friend. "You're saying another one of my friends is involved in something?"

Andrew gave a hard smile. "That I am, Bill. That I am. Now, for tonight, maybe it would be wise if you headed either home or back to the office. I would suggest home and don't come back until Monday.

You've been pulling enough long hours I need to tell you to take a break."

"Thanks, Andrew. I will. See you on Monday." Bill turned, stopped as if to say something, then shaking his head, walked away.

Andrew moved towards the cubicle where Samuel was laying. He heard quiet words and then Samuel's voice in almost anger. Pushing back the curtain, he stood for a moment, watching the three. The physician stood, hands on the end of the bed, eyes on Samuel.

"You're staying here overnight, Samuel. That's enough." Barnabas stared down his son.

Samuel finally shook his head and then regretted it as pain sliced through it. His eyes closed against the pain.

Barnabas shot a look at the physician, then at Aideen. He moved her away from the stretcher as it was moved from the cubicle.

"Andrew? You're here. What happened to Bill?" Barnabas looked behind Andrew.

"I sent him home. He's put in too many hours working this week. I talked to him. He'll behave."

"He'd better or you'll be hearing more from me." He stood, watching as the floor lights lit on the elevator panel. "What's the word on the investigation so far?"

Andrew sighed. "They didn't leave any evidence if that's what you're asking. And Samuel certainly isn't in any shape to answer questions tonight. Listen, I'll check in with him tomorrow. For tonight, I'll leave an officer on duty at his door."

"Thank you, Andrew. Come on, Aideen. Let's get my boy settled and then we'll get you home."

She stared up at him, fear in her face. "I can't stay there, Barnabas."

"No, not there. You can either use my spare room, or Andrew and his wife, Phoebe, have offered for you to stay with them for tonight."

She spun to stare at Andrew, taken aback at his smile. "I can't do that to them. I can't put them in danger." She looked between the two as they laughed.

"It's okay, Aideen. Someday, Phoebe and I will share our adventure with you. Trust me when I say it's not one you'd believe. You're welcome in our home at any time."

She nodded. "For tonight, I think I'll take up Barnabas' offer."

The two men shared at look before Andrew nodded and walked away. Aideen shoved her hands into her slacks' pockets to hide their trembling. Who had done this, she wondered? And when were they coming back?

જ⚬જ⚬જ

Samuel roused early the next morning, his headache lessened. He stared around in the dim light, wondering what had awakened him. He shook his head. Something had, but he couldn't place what it was. He raised the head of his bed, his glance going towards the windows and he saw him. The man standing here, watching him.

"Don't call for help, young man." It was an older man, his face shadowed by the hat he wore and the dim light. "I don't mean to harm you."

86

"What do you want?" Samuel's throat was dry and it made his words difficult to get out.

"I want to warn you. Someone is looking for Aideen and it seems to me they found her. Protect her." He laid a large manila envelope on the table by Samuel's bed. "Use this information to keep her safe."

"Wait! How did you get in here? I have a guard at the door."

"You do, don't you?" The man walked away, the door closing behind him.

Samuel struggled with the blankets, trying to get up, as the door opened again, and the officer stood there.

"Samuel? Who was that?"

"I was going to ask you the same thing. How'd he get in?'

"That I don't know. I was standing there the whole time and didn't see him enter." The officer walked around the room and finally opened the small closet. "I bet he's been here since before they brought you up here. He could have heard the nurses give your room number and had time to hide."

"But why stay all night?"

"Likely because you've been out of it all night. With the head injury and the painkillers, you haven't roused. The nurses have been in and out all night."

Samuel laid his head back. "You're right. The last thing I remember is talking to Andrew downstairs." He raised it again to look around. "Listen, can you find my clothes? I want to leave."

"Samuel, the doctor hasn't been by yet."

"I don't care. If you won't help, then I'll do it myself."

The officer shook his head. "Andrew will have my hide for this, you know?"

Samuel gave a small laugh as he dressed, grabbed the envelope, then headed for the door, slightly unsteady on his feet. "How many nurses are out there?"

"Enough to stop you."

"Then, we'll stop at the desk and let them know I've left."

"You're going get me into trouble, man." The officer followed on Samuel's heels, not likely this at all. He pulled out his phone and sent a text to Andrew. He knew Andrew wouldn't blame him, but he wanted it on record that Samuel had chosen to leave.

Chapter 8

Hearing a key in the lock, Barnabas looked up from the file he had been reading and watched his son enter the kitchen and sit facing him. He nodded at the officer, who left, shutting the door quietly behind him.

Samuel slid the envelope across to his father. "I had a visitor early this morning. That's why I left. He gave me this."

"A visitor? How'd he get into your room?"

"We figure he'd been there all night, waiting for me to rouse. An older man, educated I'd say from his voice. He told me to watch out for Aideen and to keep her safe."

Barnabas nodded. "And he left you that? Can you describe him at all?" When Samuel shook his head, Barnabas sat back. "Well, that certainly puts a wrinkle into it, doesn't it?"

"How's Aideen?"

"Still sleeping. It took her a while to settle down last night." He watched Samuel as his head turned towards the hall. "She's safe for now, son. Let's see what you were left."

He carefully opened the envelope and withdrew the documents and pictures inside. He sorted through them, careful in touching them.

Samuel rose to stand behind him. "Is that Aideen as a baby?"

His father nodded. "It may be. I don't think she has any photos of herself over the years to compare them to."

"It looks as if someone has been watching her throughout her entire life."

"That it does." Barnabas adjusted his reading glasses and picked up the documents as Samuel sorted through the photos. "This confirms what I've already learned. I don't see anything new here. What about the photos?"

"Try this one." Samuel handed his father a photo that had been taken in the last couple of weeks. "He followed her here, Dad. Did he send those men after us?"

"I hope not. How's the head and abdomen?"

"They hurt, but not enough to keep me down." Samuel rose, stretching as he headed for the cupboard and the coffee pot. "What now, Dad?"

"What now is that we talk to either Andrew or Bill." He gave a low laugh. "Aideen put Bill in his place last night."

"Not nice, was he?"

His father shook his head. "You know Bill when he gets an idea in his mind. He's too stubborn at times."

"He is that. Andrew reassigning the case?"

"Not that I'm aware of. He'll keep Bill on it now that he's been told to play nice." He looked towards the hallway, not hearing any sounds yet from Aideen. "We need to come up with a plan, Samuel, something that will keep both of you safe."

"Both of us?"

Barnabas nodded. "They know who you are and where you live and work. Don't think they won't come after you again. They'll keep coming until they get what they want."

Samuel sank back into his chair, his mug clinking on the tabletop, his face going even paler. "And what they want is Aideen." He looked up at his father, shadows in his eyes. "How do we keep her safe?"

"Lots of prayer for starters, son. God was there last night. You could very easily have been killed. Aideen could very easily have disappeared. Neither of those things happened."

Samuel stood, staring down at the photos, finally pulling another one out, a puzzled look on his face.

"Dad, isn't this the old library here in town?"

Barnabas took the photo, studying it. "It is. Now, why would they have that photo? The library was demolished fifteen years ago."

Samuel nodded, his head beginning to ache again. "This is strange, Dad. Does Aideen have some connection to here?"

Barnabas sat back, then shuffled quickly through the papers on the table, his hand stilling as he read. "This is why, Samuel. I'll need you to run a title search, but first, you're taking something for that headache and then heading for your old room. And don't fight me on this. You need to rest. If you don't, I'll pull you off this."

Samuel stared at his father, sighed, and reached for the painkillers he had been given. He studied the bottle, then set it down, heading instead for the medicine cabinet in the bathroom and an over-the-counter medication before flopping down on his old bed. Thoughts and ideas swirled through his head before his eyes closed and he slept. He didn't hear his father come to the door and then stand watching him before he reached for a blanket and covered his son.

Barnabas stood watching, his mind racing before he lifted his eyes. Lord, I have no idea what we're into here. I don't think I've ever felt so helpless before. I guess this is when Anna would tell me I had to trust like never before. Lord, I miss my lady. Help me to help our son.

He turned as he heard a door and then soft footsteps, walking into the hall to find Aideen standing there, staring around.

"Good morning, Aideen."

She jumped and turned, her face pale with fright. "Barnabas, I didn't see you there. Have you word on Samuel?"

Barnabas gave a wry grin as he shook his head before pointing over his shoulder. "He checked himself out over three hours ago. We've been working until I finally sent him to bed."

"He shouldn't be out yet!" Aideen moved to the doorway, the older man stepping aside to let her. "How is he?"

"Battered.   Bruised.   He won't complain but he does have a headache."

She nodded. "Did they give him any painkillers."

Barnabas gave a snort of laughter, his eyes sparkling with humour, as he pointed towards the kitchen.   "He'll not take anything.   He refuses to take heavy-duty painkillers. Always has. Sit. I'll get you some breakfast." Barnabas stood for a moment, staring at the stove, before shaking his head and moving forward. "Take a look at the photos there, Aideen. Tell me if you recognize anything."

Aideen watched him for a moment, then turned her head to study the hallway. What had she brought to them? Lord, we haven't been much on speaking terms lately, but I guess we need to be, don't we? Somewhere along the line, my faith weakened and died. I need that back.

She sorted through the photos, saying a quiet thanks when Barnabas set a plate of food beside her. She frowned, not recognizing the buildings.

"What are these buildings, Barnabas?" She looked up to find him staring down the hall towards the bedrooms.

Barnabas turned back, coming to stand beside her. He sighed, knowing he would have to let her know she likely had connections to his town.

"That's the old library, torn down a number of years ago. That's our old church. We've renovated since then, but the main building and steeple are still there. The others - they're now considered historical buildings and can't be touched. Why?"

She shrugged. "I'm just trying to understand why you got photos of buildings in town. How did you get them anyway?"

"Silas had a visitor at the hospital who left them there. That's why he's here. He checked himself out to bring them to me."

She stared up at him. "How did they manage that?"

Barnabas shrugged as he moved to sit. "We're not sure that. Now, eat. We'll talk when we're done."

Aideen suddenly shivered, feeling lost and in danger. What is it, Lord? How can I trust when I don't even have my faith any more? And don't tell me You put me through this to bring that back. Please.

જાજાજા

Samuel slowly rolled to the side of the bed and sat, scrubbing his hands down his face. He blinked at the light coming through the window. It was afternoon already, he could tell. That meant he had been asleep for hours. He stood, waiting for his balance to return, then headed for the kitchen. He needed coffee and now.

He paused as he passed the kitchen table, his hand reaching for a photo of Aideen as a teenager. He studied it, then focused more on the background, a frown in place. He knew that area, those buildings.

Barnabas stood at the back door, watching Samuel, then moved towards him.

"What do you see, son?"

Samuel stared at the picture, then tapped it. "Here. This one. Aideen in front of the Trailblazer's sign from just outside town. Dad, what's going on?"

Barnabas shook his head. "I don't know, son. Bill's on his way over. He's working this weekend after all, and I'm turning these over to him. Their lab will run them to see if they've been altered in any way or form." He ran his hand through his hair. "This is just getting so strange, Samuel. Listen, how's the head this afternoon?"

Samuel raised his eyes to watch his father. "It's better than it was but not the best. And I hurt all over."

"Expected you would be. I talked Aideen into sitting in the backyard. She's restless. Go, get yourself cleaned up and I'll make you something light to eat for now. Then, you can go join her." He watched as Samuel hesitated, then moved away. Shaking his head, he turned to look out the back door again.

Lord, what am I to do with these two? I need to keep Aideen safe but I also need to protect my son. I could sure use some ideas about now on how to do both.

Chapter 9

$\mathscr{A}$ week later, Aideen turned from the counter in the town hall and walked back outside. She looked up at the overcast sky, hoping it wouldn't rain. She had chosen to walk downtown that afternoon, probably not the best move, she thought, and she knew both men would tell her off soundly. She turned as she heard a sound, but didn't see anyone around her. She picked up her pace, hurrying to get back home before it rained.

A car slowing beside her had her moving backwards, until she realized it was one of Samuel's friends, Josiah, she thought.

"Aideen? Come on, jump in. I'll give you a ride." He shoved the passenger door open for her.

"Why?" she questioned him as she stood by the door.

"Because it's going to rain at any time and you need to get in before it does. Come on. Jump in. I need to take you home to Faith. She's been asking about you."

"She has? Again, why?"

"Because she thinks of you as a friend now and wants to get to know you better. By the way, Samuel's coming to our place for dinner tonight and the invitation included you."

She shook her head. "I'm too dangerous to know. Look what happened to Samuel."

Josiah started to laugh and Aideen spun to stare at him, shock on her face.

"Faith would have said that about herself a while ago. I didn't walk away from her. Samuel's not about to walk away from you. All the friends in our group protect one another and are there no matter what's going on."

She once more shook her head. "I have no idea what that would be like. I've always been on my own." She stared out the side window, not seeing the look of compassion that Josiah directed her way. She didn't want to see his look of pity or heard empty words.

Later that night, Samuel shut the car door after Aideen and stood, his eyes searching through the twilight. Someone was there, he knew, someone waiting for Aideen, and likely him. He turned to watch Aideen through the window, before heading around the car to slide behind the wheel.

"You've made some friends here tonight, Aideen."

She nodded, not quite sure on what had actually happened. For a few hours, she had been able to forget and just be what she always wanted to be — carefree, happy, part of a group.

"They're all sweet. Faith's little one is such a sweetheart."

"That he is. I hear tell the ladies want to get together with you on their own. Is that safe for us guys?"

She spun in the seat, staring at him, before catching the spark of mischief in his eyes.

"I would think so, unless there's something you want to confess."

He shook his head, realizing she had found him out. "Nope. Not tonight. Say, have you heard from Bill this week?"

"I heard early this afternoon from him. The lab's had a chance to look at the photos. They're not doctored in any way that they can see. That means I really was here in Elmton at some point. But did I live here or just visit?"

"Dad's digging into that. I've been looking through titles on the buildings in the photos. I found some interesting stuff that I need to talk to you and Dad about and then pass on to Bill." He paused, not quite sure how to ask the next question. "About Bill? He's been okay with you?"

She nodded. "He apologized, you know. I think Andrew put him up to that. But he's been fine. I gather from what he told me, they're swamped with investigations, but Bill has something else going on. Something in his personal life. Has he said anything to you?"

Samuel shook his head, wondering where this was going. "Did he to you?"

"No. It's just an impression I got. He's unsettled, Samuel. Something has him upset and it's not work. One of you should talk to him."

"I will. I can't think what it would be though." He pulled into the driveway and turned off the car. "Listen, I want to meet with Dad in the morning. You up for a breakfast meeting? I know he has to fly out tomorrow afternoon for a court case."

"I can be. Here or your Dad's?"

"Dad's, I think." He waited until she unlocked the door and turned off the security system. "I'll see you around 8 tomorrow morning."

༄ঌ·ঌঌ·ঌঌ

Barnabas waved at the two the next morning as they entered his kitchen, his phone cradled between his ear and shoulder as he scribbled on a pad of paper. Aideen stood staring at him for a moment, then sighing, moved towards the counter. She studied what he had out, then worked to prepare their breakfast, sliding French toast and fresh fruit onto plates and then in front of the men. Samuel stood, pulling back her chair and hand on her shoulder making her

104

sit. He reached for the juice and coffee, sitting both on the table.

Barnabas finally ended his call and bowed his head for a moment, before picking up his fork.

"This is good, Aideen. Not what I had planned."

"And what had you planned?"

"Not telling. That way, next time it will be a surprise."

"Next time, huh? Now spill. Samuel says you have information."

Samuel choked on his coffee. "Whoa! Slow down, Aideen. Let's eat first, okay?"

She smacked him on his arm. "You're the one who told me your Dad had information. Now, you want me to wait? Make up your mind, buddy."

Barnabas lowered his head to hide his smile. These two were acting like more than just friends, and he liked what he say. Aideen had become like a daughter to him and he wanted to keep her in the family. She was good for Samuel, and he was for her.

"Samuel's right, Aideen. Let's eat first. Then I want us to spend some time in prayer. What I have found out is a game-changer and also a life-changer for you. I need to get through it before I have to leave and I know you'll have lots of questions. Andrew's coming by as well, as I wanted someone else here."

Aideen froze, her eyes fixed on Barnabas. "Is it that bad?"

"No, not necessarily. Now, eat up. Andrew's to be here by nine, and I'm expecting another call before that."

Aideen stood, her hands in the soapy dishwater, eyes on the suds. Samuel stood beside her, dish towel in hand, waiting for the plate she was scouring. He finally reached for it, startling her.

"Sorry, Aideen, but I don't think you can scrub that design off. I think it's baked into the plate."

She stared at his hand, then looked up at him, tears sparkling in her eyes. He sighed, then reached to pull her into a hug.

"I don't know what Dad found, but we'll walk through it with you, okay? You're not on your own. Never again."

Andrew stood for a moment watching them, then nodded. Phoebe was right, he thought. There's something there all right.

"Samuel. Aideen. Good morning. Your Dad around?"

Samuel looked over his shoulder at Andrew. "He is. He took a call in the office. There's coffee if you want. We're just finishing up the breakfast dishes."

"I can see that." Andrew's voice held a touch of amusement, and Samuel's eyes narrowed as he stared as his friend. "Where does your Dad want to meet?"

"The office, but he'll come find us, he said. Any word on my assailants?" He moved back from Aideen and handed her some tissues.

"Not yet. Whoever they were, they were good. They didn't leave any trace evidence that we could find, but it's difficult to know as there are people in and out of your office all the time."

"That's true."

Barnabas stood for a moment in the doorway, papers in hand, before he spoke.

"Let's get to it then, shall we? I have three hours before I have to leave for the airport and it's going to take close to that."

Andrew nodded. "I gather you've found a wealth of information then."

"I have, and it's disturbing, Andrew, very disturbing."

Aideen tried hard to absorb the information Barnabas was throwing at them and the questions and answers the three men were working through. She was numb, hearing that she was from that town, had been back there many times over the years but not recognizing anything about it. How did that happen?

Andrew watched her, seeing the conflict going on with her. He finally rose and came to sit beside her on the couch.

"Aideen? Talk to us."

She shook her head. "I don't know what to say, Andrew. I can't take all this in. I just don't understand it."

"We know you don't. We don't expect you to."

"But just what does it all mean?" She searched the faces of the three men.

"It means that we need to do more digging, Aideen. You're somehow connected to this town, and we need to figure out how. Whoever is behind this will likely stop at nothing. Andrew here is accessing the records about your parents. Samuel here will keep you as safe as he can. I've to be out of town for four days, but I'll work on it as I can." Barnabas paused, not quite sure how to phrase the next comment. "Have you ever had a boyfriend, been engaged, Aideen? We need to rule out someone like that."

She shook her head. "No, never. No one wanted to go out with me. I'm the girl from the wrong side of town, the foster child everyone looked down on." She studied her hands, trying to control her tears. "I would see the other foster kids dating, the kids from school, but I was always the one standing on the sidelines, watching."

Andrew and Barnabas shared a quick look before Barnabas looked at his son. He nodded. Samuel's heart was not quite on his sleeve but it was close.

"That's one thing we don't have to worry about then. No stalkers, no one like that?" When she shook her head, he continued. "Hear me out, you two. Andrew and I have talked at length about what I am to say. If either of you say no, then we bring in a police officer to be with you at all times." Aideen's eyes were closed to Barnabas. "Aideen, what happened yesterday proves someone is out to find you. We are absolutely sure you are an only child. We have proof of that. We have proof as well about your parents' deaths. It's part of the investigation and once Andrew has Bill confirm some facts for him, he'll talk to you about that. For the present, Aideen, I want you to move into this house. It has an even better security system than where you are now." He watched her closely. "We are also asking that you go nowhere on your own. If Samuel or I can't be with you, we want you to contact Andrew. He will have someone there."

"People will talk, Dad." Samuel finally spoke.

"I know they will, but they'll talk even more if Aideen stays in the apartment. At least here, the talk can be minimized."

Samuel nodded at that. "One further step we may need to take. I want the two of you to think very carefully about it over the next few days that I'm away and give me your answer then. Don't talk to one another about it. Spend time in prayer." He paused, and the two watched him. "Samuel, we're going to be asking you to put your life on the line here, son. Aideen, what we're asking is not done lightly. Think about posing at a couple for now. That may bring out whoever is behind this." He held up his hand as Aideen went to speak. "No. Don't answer now. Wait until I'm back. With that, I need to go. Andrew's your go-to person for now."

Aideen stared at him, shaking her head. "That won't work."

Barnabas held up his finger. "No, not today, Aideen. I've given you a timeline to think and pray about it. Samuel, you have five friends you can go to and talk to. I encourage you to do that. Andrew here, he can give you advice from more than one point of view. Aideen, I know you'll want to talk to someone. Any one of the wives will help, but I would first suggest Phoebe,

Andrew's wife. She has quite a tale to tell you."

Aideen finally looked at Samuel, catching him watching her, an unreadable look on his face. "Thank you, Barnabas. I'll consider that."

Andrew looked up at Barnabas. "You're needing to leave. I'm off today. What do you say, Samuel, you and Aideen come with me?   Phoebe wants to meet Aideen. We can spend the day quietly at our place. You and I can talk, if you want."

Aideen finally nodded, then rose to hug Barnabas. She turned without a word, the three men watching her. Samuel went to say something, then holding up his hand, headed for the backyard.

Andrew looked in the directions they had gone, then spoke. "That went about how you expected it to go, didn't it?"

Barnabas nodded. "It did. That's why I put a timeline on it and asked them to pray out but not talk to one another.   Come Thursday when I get back, we'll sit down again and then I'll send them off to talk." He turned. "Listen, I need to get going. If you need me, call."

"I'll do that. Just so you know, Lily's agreed to come and stay with Phoebe here for the next few days. I think it will do Aideen good."

"Lily? Wonderful. Now if we could only work on Aideen's faith."

"She's struggling, my friend, because of what she's gone through all her life. We need to cover her in prayer."

❧❧❧

Phoebe watched as Aideen walked across the grass towards her. Somewhere along the line, Aideen had lost her shoes and was savouring the feel of the grass on her feet. She had not been allowed to do that as a child and took every opportunity to do just that now. She slipped into the chair beside Phoebe and leaned back, enjoying the shade.

"Phoebe? Can I ask you something?"

"Sure." Phoebe sipped her juice, then looked over at Aideen. "Andrew told me what Barnabas asked of you and Samuel. Talk to me."

Aideen shrugged. "I know why he did it, but it puts Samuel at such risk. I can feel someone around me, watching me all the

113

time. I have glimpses of them. Everywhere I go, I'm so afraid."

Phoebe nodded. "I used to be like that, for the four or five months before I married Andrew. In fact, it came out I had been stolen when I was really young. The people who raised me were responsible. I had no freedom. Even the work I was doing as an adult was arranged by my mother." She watched as Aideen started, then stared at her. "I was kidnapped a few months ago, beaten until I was afraid to even open my mouth. Andrew was asked to find me and rescue me." She smiled as she remembered. "He did just that. Came into the roadhouse I was being held in, swept me away on his motorbike. The next day, Silas suggested that I change my name to protect myself and hide, and Andrew and I married. We had quite the adventure until the men and women responsible were caught. I've had a chance to reunite with my biological family. We're slowing building a relationship again."

"You would never know, Phoebe. You hadn't met Andrew before?" When Phoebe shook her head, Aideen sighed, then sat back. "I don't know what to do, Phoebe. I don't want to put Samuel at risk, but I can't continue living like I am."

"No, you can't. So you have a couple of options. One is that you run and I can guarantee you won't get far. That man over there will come looking for you. Two is that you can hide but that won't stop them from looking for you. Three is that you make a stand and that includes posing as Samuel's sweetheart."

Aideen's head jerked up at that. "That's would it would be, wouldn't it? Oh, I couldn't do that. I'm sure he already has a girlfriend."

Phoebe shook her head. "No, he doesn't. He's never been one to date. Andrew can't remember him going on a date as long as he's known him and that's all his life. He'll be part of a group of friends that go out, will socialize at church, but that's it. In case you're wondering, each of our friends who are married have a similar tale to tell. You may want to talk to them as well."

"No, I don't think I'll need to. Your story was wild enough!" Aideen's hands covered her mouth. "I'm sorry. That's wasn't nice."

Phoebe laughed so hard she had to set her glass down. "You should have lived it, Aideen. It was pretty wild. Imagine being married, learning to care for someone, and not able to verbalize your feelings until he's threatened. That's what happened." Her eyes traced across the yard to where her husband stood, her eyes softening. "I know it was God, Aideen. It had to be. Andrew's not the type to do what he did, but he did it willingly. He told me afterwards he fell in love with my picture."

Aideen sat back. "I'm just so afraid, Phoebe."

"I know you are. We'll keep you in our prayers. But now this. If Samuel does agree to this and if I know my friend, he will, he will walk into it having prayed about it enough to have peace, and he'll do it not because he has to but because he wants to. I can see how he looks at you."

Andrew watched the two women talking and turned to Samuel.

"Samuel?"

Samuel shook his head. "What? Oh, what Dad asked. It's not fair to Aideen, Andrew."

"Is being dead fair to her?"

Samuel's eyes shot to his. "What do you mean?"

"Just what I said. Is it fair to refuse to do what your Dad asked and have Aideen dead?"

Samuel shrugged, then sighed. "No. I just don't know, Andrew. I've never dated, never felt like I wanted to."

"But now you do, and it has nothing to do with keeping Aideen alive." Andrew grinned at the look he got. "You know that as well as I do. You're beginning to care for that lady over there."

"I am, but how do I do this?"

"How did I do it when Phoebe and I ended up married? One day at a time, Samuel. Just one day at a time. Lots of prayer, too. Your Dad wouldn't have asked if he had any other way. He's given you time to think about it and pray about it. Maybe this is how Aideen will regain her faith."

Samuel stared at him, then nodded. "I hear what you're saying but I'm still not convinced it's the right way."

"Does your head and the bruises not tell you that? Next time, you or Aideen may not get off so lucky."

Samuel stared at the women, then nodded. "I know. I just wish there was another way. I don't want to force Aideen into anything she may not want to be in."

Andrew sighed. "Then you have a lot of work ahead of you. I can see you two together, but you both need to agree on this. If you don't, then your Dad will stick her way somewhere with a security team and not let you near her at all. He won't even tell you where she is. Can you live with that?"

Samuel ran his hands through his hair, leaving his hands clasped behind his head, as he thought over what Andrew had said. "Let me think and pray about it. Dad's home on Thursday. Can we meet sometime on Wednesday?"

"We can. I'll be around the department. How be we meet for supper here? Phoebe has a college class that night so we'd be on our own."

"That works. Thanks, Andrew."

Chapter 10

*Th*ursday morning finally came. Samuel sank into his office chair and sat, head in hands, for a while. He finally roused and turned to his work, hearing Aideen moving quietly about the office. Finally, he gave up trying to work. He need to talk to her.

"Aideen, can you come in for a moment?" When she appeared at the door, he pointed to a chair. "Sit, please. We need to talk."

She nodded, her eyes on the floor. She knew what she wanted. She just wasn't sure if it was the right thing to do.

"Aideen?" Samuel's voice was quiet. When she didn't look up, he sighed and came around to sit beside her, reaching for her hand.

She jumped at his touch before looking up at him.

"We do need to talk." At her nod, he continued, "We've both spent the last few days in prayers. I made a list of pros and cons. I've talked it over with Andrew again, and I know what I want to do."

Aideen laid her fingers on his mouth. "Before you say anything more, I've prayed about it. Phoebe and I have talked. I've talked to Faith and Julia and heard Paige and Larkin's stories as well. I know what I want to do, but I don't think it's fair or safe for you. I still feel the men out there, following us, just waiting for the right opportunity."

"They are." Samuel hesitated, at loss for words. "I know what I want to do, Aideen. If you are willing, will you be my girl? I don't mean just for this. I really want to go out with you. This is getting in our way."

Aideen started to laugh and then couldn't stop at the look on his face. She finally sobered enough to nod. "That's my line, buddy. What'd you do, read my mind?"

Samuel stared at her for a moment, then began to laugh. "I guess God told us, huh? So, how be we work away and then go for lunch together?"

She shook her head. "No. We finish off the day's work, and then we go talk to your Dad. I want to find out what more he's found out and why particularly he wants us to pose as if we're dating. He's not doing it just to get us together."

Samuel thought about that. "You're right. Okay, then, Miss Secretary. It's back to work for both of us."

Barnabas turned as he heard his back door open and the younger couple entered. Aideen came up beside him and dropped a kiss on his cheek, then moved him aside so she could work on the salad he had started. Barnabas shook his head and reached instead for the chicken he had ready for the grill, throwing up his hands when Samuel reached it first.

"Okay, you two. What are you two up to?"

Samuel just smiled as he headed out the door. He could hear Aideen asking about the court case but he couldn't make out his father's responses. He stopped as he reached for the grill and set the chicken down carefully.   There was a note on the table at the side of it.

"Dad!   I think you need to get out here!"

Barnabas was at his side in a few strides, searching Samuel's face, then the area he had pointed at. He reached for the note, then stopped, heading back inside for gloves. Opening the letter, he stepped back a moment his eyes studying his son.

"What decision did you two come to?"

Samuel stared at him for a moment, then past him at Aideen standing behind his father.

"We were going to talk to you tonight but we were going to be seen as a couple. Why?"

Barnabas nodded as he turned to Aideen.   "That's what you agreed to? Where were you when you had this discussion?"

"In Samuel's office."   Aideen's voice died away. "No. Don't tell me." Her head was shaking in the negative.

"Somehow they've found out about it. We'll need to have Andrew or Bill sweep your office, son. This note indicates that they know what you're planning, and that it won't stop them. They're threatening both of you as well." He paused, then reached for his phone. "We need to call this in. Samuel, you might as well grill all that chicken. We'll be having company for supper. Aideen, is the salad large enough?"

The two stared at the older man for a moment, then turned to do what he had asked. Barnabas stared around his yard. Even here Aideen wasn't safe, nor was Samuel. And he could put in a pretty good guess that he wouldn't be either.

☙☙☙

Bill stood, staring down at the note, not quite comprehending what it was about, before he looked at the three in front of him.

"What's this about? You two are a couple now?"

Barnabas nodded. "It's a ploy, Bill, to try and bring the culprits out of the woodwork. It looks as if it's working."

"And who all knew about this?" Bill was angry and felt he had a right to be.

"Andrew was in on the planning of it, so take your anger up with him. Other than Phoebe, we were the only ones who knew it was a ploy. Aideen talked to a couple of other ladies, but they didn't know anything other than Aideen was feeling out about Samuel." Barnabas reached and tapped the plastic bag. "Now, what do we do about that?"

"How would I know? It sounds as if you three and Andrew are planning things without letting anyone else in on it."

"Bill, that is enough and unwarranted. If I have to I'll speak to Andrew once more and have you permanently removed from this case. Don't make the mistake of thinking I won't. You've already been warned."

Bill nodded. "I apologize, Barnabas. Now, where are they?"

"In the living room. I didn't want them in the yard until your team had swept it."

Bill nodded once more and then sighed. What was it with his friends? Couldn't they be safe no how?

Samuel watched as Aideen moved restlessly around the back deck a few days later, finally walking towards her.

"Come on. Let's go get ice cream or coffee or something?"

She nodded. "I don't like this, Samuel."

"I know you don't. Neither do I. But we have to still live our lives. Now, let's go, okay?"

She shrugged, finally walking ahead of him to his car. Once downtown, they headed for a nearby park, almost deserted. Aideen searched for a bench, finally sitting down on one quite a ways from the road.

"Why here, Aideen?"

"I didn't know. I just don't to be close to the road." She looked around, not feeling safe. "Someone's out there, Samuel. I can feel him." She jumped as she saw the two men approaching, hoods up and sunglasses in place.

They stopped in front of the two, and Samuel made to rise, prevented from doing so by hands on his shoulders. He reached for Aideen's hand as he stared at the two men.

"We don't mean to harm you. Sorry we scared you, Aideen."

"How do you know my name?" She looked between the two men, then at Samuel.

"We know more than what you think we do. We're from this town. We need your help, Samuel. Here's a list of properties you need to search through. They were given faulty inspections and this needs to be addressed. Here's also a list of names that go with them. We need you to search this out and bring the culprits to justice."

Samuel refused to take the paper. "Why don't you go to the authorities yourself?"

"We can't." The second man searched Samuel's face. "Our purpose is to bring justice to our town from behind the scenes. You two have been chosen to help. What you are involved in personally is linked to this." The paper was dropped on the bench beside Samuel, and the men walked away.

Samuel spun to search for the one who had been behind him, but that man was already gone. He had faded into the shrubbery, pulling down his hood as he watched. He sighed, knowing that the investigation was far from over, and then turned to make his way out of town.

Aideen stared around, then at Samuel.

"Did that really just happen?"

He nodded, then grasping her hand, pulled her to her feet and across to his car, slamming the door behind her. He slid behind the wheel, papers in his hand, and headed for his father's.

"What was on those papers, Samuel?"

"I'm not sure. I'll have to search, I guess, but I want Dad to see them. I need to hear what he has to say."

Samuel slapped on his brakes as the car in front of them stopped suddenly. His eyes narrowed, he reached for Aideen's hand. "We should hide these papers, Aideen. I don't like this, not one bit."

She nodded. "Okay but where?" Then she slipped off her shoes, folding the papers as thinly as she could before slipping then under the insoles and then the shoes back on her feet.

Samuel watched as the doors to the car ahead of them opened. He reached for the shifter and sent the car into reverse, spinning the wheel at the same time to send them in the opposite direction. He sped off, eyes flicking to the rearview mirror. He finally breathed a sigh of relief.

"We've gotten away from them, but now we have to get home." He pulled to the side of the road and called his father. "Voice mail. He must be on the phone."

"Call 911, then, and get an escort."

"No. I don't want to do that. Not until I'm sure of what we were given."

She nodded, then reached for his phone. "Keep driving. I'll keep trying to reach your Dad."

"But where do we drive to, Aideen? They know where we both live. They know where we work. They've already proven they don't really care if one of us gets hurt."

"No. They've proven they don't care if you get hurt. If this goes back as far as your Dad thinks, then I'm not at risk. Not yet anyway."

Samuel nodded. "That's true, but I do need to find somewhere to keep you safe." He looked around. "Let's leave my car here. We can get around on foot a lot easier."

"Really? A lot easier? And just were are getting around to?" Her voice was testy. She was exhausted, and it showed. She sat staring out the car window. Finally, she spoke. "Take me home, Samuel. It doesn't seem to matter about anything any more."

Samuel stared at her for a moment before he put the car in gear. Did she just give up, Lord? How do I reach her? He didn't like the resignation he saw in her face. She wasn't fighting any more. He followed her into his Dad's home, watching as she headed for her bedroom, not saying anything. He then went looking for his father.

"Dad? Anything new?"

Barnabas looked up, his eyes on his son's face. "Sit. Tell me what happened."

Samuel did, ending his words with a sigh. "I just don't understand, Dad. She's giving up."

"It looks that way, son, but I don't think she is. She's overwhelmed right at the moment with everything that's going on. Don't change how you react with her. She needs the stability of your friendship." He sat back, his eyes on the doorway. "I wish I knew better how to tell you to react. Now, about these men? Did you recognize anything about them?"

Samuel shook his head. "Not really, just the sense that I knew who they were." He rose and began pacing. "Aideen has the papers." He headed for the kitchen and found the shoes she had kicked off, pulling out the papers before heading back to the office. "This is what they gave me."

Barnabas took the papers and studied them before rising and heading for his bookshelf. "Here's an old town directory. Take a look through it and see if you recognize anything in it."

Chapter 11

A week later, Aideen rose from her desk and headed for the door. She was restless and didn't quite know why. She just couldn't sit there any longer. Samuel was out of the office, and she knew he wouldn't be happy if she left. He'll have to get over it, she thought, as she locked the door and headed for the car she had been using. She needed some time by herself. She wasn't used to being around people all the time. She just needed to go somewhere and she had no idea where.

She finally pulled into a parking lot, staring at the building in front of her. Why had she ended up at the church, she wondered, staring at the solid looking white church, her eyes tracing up to the steeple. She finally opened her door and after locking the car, wandered to the cemetery, her eyes reading the names, but not really taking them in. She finally stopped as a long-forgotten name caught her attention. She reached to trace it. It was her last name, but she didn't know who it was.

A sound to her left started her and she jumped, turning to find the pastor of the church, Silas Peters, standing near her, just watching.

"I'm sorry, Aideen. I didn't mean to startle you." He walked across the grass towards her. "Did you find someone you recognize?"

"This is my name, but I don't know who this is. I have no idea how I'm connected to this town, but it seems I am."

"That's what I've been hearing, Aideen. Do you want to talk about it?" He pointed towards the trees where a bench had been situated.

"Thank you. Maybe I should. I'm too close to the situation with Samuel and even Barnabas. I don't know Andrew well enough to talk to him."

Silas nodded as they walked across the grass. He waited until they were sitting before sliding around to face her. "Okay, so tell me. What really brought you here?"

She sighed. "I'm not sure. I was just driving around, trying to get it all clear in my head, and ended up here. Now, you tell me why."

"God." She threw him a look and he grinned at her. "God knew you needed to come here. Not necessarily to talk to me but to see that gravestone. Now, maybe you'll get some answers."

"I don't know, Silas. I don't even know the questions."

"You don't, but God does. He also knows the answers." He waited. "How's your faith?"

She snorted. "Not great. I can't say it ever has been." She looked up at the sky, tears sparkling in her eyes. "I used to pray for a family of my own, for my foster parents to be nicer. I used to pray to die too. God never answered any of my prayers."

"But you see, He did." That comment brought Aideen's eyes to his, a frown on her face. "God doesn't always give us what we want. He gives us what we need. For you, it was the foster parents. They have made you a stronger person, put you through circumstances that you can use to help someone else. I can't see you as a secretary for life, not unless you find something else to complement it."

"I know. I would hate to walk out on Samuel, but I might have to. I might have to, just to keep him safe."

Silas nodded, knowing that she was finally working through what she had to. "Let me pray with you. Then, we can talk more, or I can leave and let you just sit here and be still in God's presence. This is where you'll need to find the faith to trust God, to know He had a plan and purpose for your life. It's hard to do, I know from personal experience, but it's doable."

She nodded, then watched as he finally walked away, her thoughts confused. She finally rose and headed for her car, her eyes on the sky, not watching where she was heading.

***

"Dad, have you seen Aideen?" Samuel walked into his father's office late that afternoon.

"No." Barnabas looked up from the files he was working on. "Isn't she at work?"

135

Samuel shook his head. "No, she's not. It looks as if she took off early. No note or anything to say where she was."

"I don't like this, son." He rose. "Any idea where she might have gone?"

Samuel shook his head. "None whatsoever. She knows we want her to wait for one of us to bring her back and forth to work. The thing is the car she was using is gone."

"Okay. So, we start searching. Call Bill and let him know. Give him the plate number as well." Barnabas reached for his keys. "Here, leave a note for her in case she comes back."

The men headed in opposite directions, aimlessly driving around, trying to find Aideen or her vehicle. Finally, Samuel's phone rang.

"Samuel? It's Bill. A patrol officer found her car. It's at the church, but she's not in it."

"The church? That's odd."

"You mean, she wouldn't have gone there?"

"I mean, it's not like her to have. Is Silas around?"

"I have Lily looking for him. He's not home."

"Try the high school. I think this is the night he usually works at the gym there with the basketball team."

"Right. I forgot. I'll send Lily that way. I gather you're heading this way."

"I am. Just let me call Dad and let him know."

Barnabas stood by his car for a moment, his eyes watchful, before he looked at his son. He sighed. Aideen, where are you? You're tearing my boy apart, you know. Lord, protect her wherever she is. Only You know at this point in time.

"Dad?" Samuel's voice roused him.

"Son. Any word?"

Samuel shook his head. "Not yet. The lab team is going over the car, but it's still locked up with her purse inside it. Silas says he spoke with her for about thirty minutes about mid-afternoon. He found her staring at one of the gravestones."

"He did? First, let's go talk with Bill and see what he has to say. Then I want to talk to Silas, to find out what he says. Did you get a chance to run any of those searches?"

Samuel nodded. "It just gets deeper and deeper, Dad. What I have found out is that one of the founding families is behind a lot of building and that building is the one with the shoddy inspections."

"About what I thought you'd find out." He looked up as they approached Bill.

"Bill, any word?" Samuel's voice was hopeful.

Bill turned, shaking his head. "It looks as if she just locked up and walked away. Silas is on his way back. He had to find someone to cover for him." He peered at Samuel, shaking his head. Not another one, please, dear Lord.

Samuel stared around. "Did Silas say what gravestone it was?"

"No, he didn't. He said he's show us when he got here. The team's about finished. They didn't find a lot. Oh. They asked if you would take Aideen's purse,

138

though. They said there's no money in it and her debit card is missing."

Barnabas nodded. "Tell them to put it into my car and lock the doors." He turned as he hear tires on the gravel parking lot. "There's Silas now."

Silas walked slowly towards them, his eyes turning from one to the other before centring on Samuel.

"Samuel. Any word?"

Samuel shook his head. "None. I don't know if that's Aideen's normal course or not, though. I don't know if she'd run."

"I would say she wouldn't. Rather, she'd shut down and bury herself deep inside. We had an interesting talk this afternoon. Come with me. I'll show you the gravestone she was looking at."

Samuel and Barnabas exchanged a look as they say the name.

"I didn't see this coming." Barnabas shook his head as he realized the implications of this. "Samuel, those searches you're running. Did you come across this name?"

"I did. I didn't realize it would be connected to Aideen. O'Rourke is a common name here in the cemetery. I remember that from running through here as a kid."

"I did some research on this one after Aideen and I talked. It's one of the founding families, but a different branch than Aideen's family would have been. From what I can see, this branch of the family was into criminal activities." Silas spoke up.

Barnabas nodded. "I remember that. I just never connected Aideen to them, I guess because she was raised elsewhere. I just pray this oversight hasn't harmed her."

"Dad, please. You're tied up in so many investigations right now. You have to leave again for another court case in two days. We'll work on this."

Barnabas nodded. "I know I do. I'm going to ask a friend to take over the investigation of Aideen's family. I'm getting too close."

Samuel shook his head. "I don't see that, Dad." He turned, shoulders slumping as he walked away, the three men who had been with him watching, their thoughts dark and muddled.

Three weeks later, Samuel stuffed his paperwork into an envelope, sealed it, addressed it, then rummaged through his desk for stamps. Finding now, he rose and headed for Aideen's desk, stopping for a moment. He shook his head. He felt like she was there but she wasn't. He found the stamps and then the day's mail. Sorting through it, he stopped at a plain white envelope that had one word written on it. His name and in Aideen's handwriting.

"Samuel"

His hand froze for a moment, before he picked it up, staring around the office and then heading for the door. No sign of her. He locked the office, heading for his home.

"Samuel,

"if you are reading this, then I have had to make the decision to step away from you and your Dad. It has become too dangerous. I can't let either of you put yourselves at risk any more.

141

"You will have found the car and know what gravestone I was looking at. Use that, Samuel, to find the information you need to put these men away. I have had to go into hiding to protect myself and more importantly to protect you. They are watching everyone I have had contact with. I can't let them hurt you.

"Please do not try and find me. I haven't left town as I am sure Bill has let you know. He's been watching for just that. There is one person I have been in contact with one person and only one. I will not tell you who. It is too risky.

"Please, Samuel, forgive me. I took your heart with me, I know, but left you mine. If the Lord wills, we will be together again. I am looking for the information I need that will bring these men and yes women to justice. When I have that, I will contact your father, not you. They have too close an eye on you. I have taken a chance just to leave this for you.

"Keep your trust, my love. God has you in His hands. Your faith has shown me back to where I need to be. If this is

the only thing I could leave with you,
know that this is the truth. I have seen
where God is every step of this walk, now
that my eyes are opened.

"Know too that I love you. I pray
that we will grow old together, but it is
only as God allows.

"Aideen"

Samuel drew in a deep breath. This
was not what he had expected. His eyes
traced the words again. Where was she,
Lord? I need to find her and I can't.

Chapter 12

*B*arnabas watched as his son paced the living room that evening. Something had happened, but Samuel hadn't said what.

"What's going on, son?"

Samuel paused, his eyes going up to the ceiling before he spoke. "Aideen's still in town, Dad. She's looking for the men."

Barnabas slowly nodded. That was the conclusion he had come to. "And how do you know this?"

"She left me a letter today in the office. I don't know how she got in and out without me seeing her, unless she gave it to the mailman and he said she didn't. She doesn't want me to look for her any more."

"That won't stop you." Barnabas rose and approached his son. "What else?"

Samuel shrugged. "Just some personal stuff, Dad."

"Do we need to talk to Andrew or Bill?"

Samuel turned, his eyes thoughtful. "I'm not sure, Dad. She said she's been in contact with one person. She wouldn't say who."

Barnabas nodded, having a good idea who it was. "Then, we'll just continue as we have been. I'll continue to search through what I have. Paul's searching as well. You continue your searches on the titles."

"I'm almost through them all now, Dad, unless more come up. I'm ready to turn over what I have to Bill tomorrow. I'm supposed to meet him at the department." He paused, his thoughts going to the letter. "Wait. Maybe's that not such a good idea."

"Tomorrow's Friday, Samuel. Take it with you to church on Sunday. If you have to, leave it with Silas. He'll make sure it gets to either Bill or Andrew."

"That might be a good plan, Dad. I left a copy of what I have on your desk, just in case mine goes missing. I guess I'll see you later next week, then."

"Good thought. I'll lock it in the safe. And yes, I fly out tonight for five days."

With a nod of thanks, Samuel walked away, out into the night. He drove to his home, his eyes watchful. He didn't see the man who rose from hiding near his deck. He felt the cloth bag go over his head but before he could fight back against the arms holding him, he felt a prick and seconds later his vision blurred and his body grew limp. A few whispered words and he was carried to a waiting car and stuffed inside.

Aideen watched in horror from her hiding place near the garage. This couldn't be happening. She scurried to the end of the house, frantically searching for a pen as she mouthed the plate number of the vehicle. Her wrist would have to do as a piece of paper. Then she sank to the ground, her arms wrapped around her legs, head on her knees as she wept. They took Samuel because they couldn't find her. She raised her head, blinking to clear her eyes. Who could she go to? She rose and headed away from the house. She didn't want them to find her and she was sure someone would have stayed behind just for that reason.

The church finally came into view. She hesitated, not quite sure if this was the right step, then moved forward, her head twisting as she searched for someone lurking, someone who would grab her and have her disappear. She still hadn't got it all figured out, though, as to why.

Silas looked up from his studies as he heard the church door softly close. He frowned, looking at the clock. No one should be here. He rose, heading for the sanctuary. His footsteps slowed as he reached the hallway.

"Aideen?" His head tilted, he studied her for a moment. "You're here. What's happened?"

She shook her head as tears flowed once more. Her mouth opened as if to speak, but no words came.

Silas walked towards her, hand outstretched. "Come, Aideen. Let's get you sitting down." He led her back to his office and almost shoved her into a chair. "Now. Tell me what's going on."

She shook her head, her emotions not letting her speak. Silas sighed, then took a second look at her feet. He headed out of his office, returning with a basin of warm water and towels. He knelt, removing her shoes and placing her feet into the water. He then reached for a bottle of water from his fridge.

"Here, drink this. I'm going to try and reach Andrew. He needs to know you are here." He watched her closely as he pulled out his phone, making the call. "I'm glad you came here, Aideen. Were you followed?"

She looked up, then shook her head. "I don't think I was. They would have picked me up if they had been following me." She shuddered. "It's a long walk from Samuel's home."

Silas choked back a groan. He had not expected her to walk. Since he was the only one she had kept in contact with, he had expected her to call him. "Why didn't you call me?"

She shook her head again. "I couldn't. I don't want to place you in any danger."

"That's not what our agreement was, Aideen. You agreed to call me if you needed anything." He looked up at the sound of the church door closing and stood. "Stay here. I'll be right back."

Silas slipped the lock on the door as he closed it before heading down the office hallway. He stood for a moment, watching as Andrew paced in the entryway.

"Andrew? Thanks for coming."

Andrew looked up as Silas approached him. "You said it was important." He eyed his friend and pastor. "So, what's the deal?"

Silas sighed, knowing Andrew would not be happy. "I have Aideen locked in my office." He held up his hand as Andrew went to speak. "Before you say anything, listen. Okay? Aideen approached me about three weeks ago, asking for help. She refused to contact you or Bill. She was adamant she wanted to stay in hiding to protect Samuel and Barnabas." He paused. "As she had come to me as a member of the congregation, I agreed, with the stipulation that if I felt it warranted, I would contact you and tell you where she was, hoping she hadn't moved on me."

"And you didn't."

"No. She's fragile right now, Andrew, and what was going on was enough to tip her over emotionally. She was only to stay in hiding for two weeks. She hasn't contacted me in the last two weeks. Today, she showed up her. I have no idea why. But she did walk from Samuel's house to here."

"She walked?" Andrew ran his hands through his hair before staring at Silas. "That's quite the walk."

Silas pointed back towards his office. "She's really on the edge right now. She hasn't said what happened, but it had to be something big for her to be here. I think she's been crying the whole way."

"Something happen to Samuel?" Andrew's voice quieted as they neared the door.

Silas shrugged. "I did try to reach him but it went straight to voice mail."

Andrew pulled out his own phone. "I'll have Bill or Jason drop by and see if Samuel's around. Barnabas just flew out of town tonight." He sighed. "I was hoping this would have been over all ready."

"You and me both. Samuel was looking ragged on Sunday. He's worried about Aideen. I couldn't say anything. With her coming in this way, she was looking for help." Silas unlocked his door. Before opening it, he commented. "I have her soaking her feet. She's got some nice blisters."

"So, do we need to find medical help for her?"

Silas shook his head. "Not quite yet. I think you need to hear what she has to say first."

Andrew stood for a moment, watching Aideen. He could see how fragile she was. He slipped into the chair beside her, not saying anything.

She looked up at him, then back down, swiping at the tears on her face. He sighed, rose and went to find a small towel he could dampen. He handed it to her and sat again, waiting for her to talk.

"They took Samuel, Andrew."

Whatever it was that he had expected her to say, it wasn't that. He shot a look at Silas, then back at her.

"When?"

"Before I came here. I didn't have a phone to call you. I thought Silas could."

"He did. But that's quite a while ago, Aideen."

She nodded, the tears falling again. "I know. Here's the plate number." She held out her arm so he could read what she had written.

Pulling out his phone, he made the call, then watched her again, seeing what Silas had meant.

"Aideen, can you tell me anything about the men at all?"

She nodded. "I didn't see much as I tried to stay hidden. There were two. One dressed in black, the other in camouflage. They put a bag or something over his head and then he just seemed to go limp. I don't know why. It was a smaller gray car, four door. I'm sorry, I don't know the make or year."

"That's okay. Did you notice anything else?"

She shook her head. "No. I was just so upset about what happened." She looked up at Andrew. "I shouldn't have gone into hiding. They wouldn't have gone after Samuel."

"No. I think they would have anyway. They did before, remember?" Andrew sighed as he pulled out his phone and read the text, his mouth tightening as he did so.

"Silas, I need to run, but we need to get Aideen somewhere safe." Frowning, he thought through where he could place her.

"How about I worry about that?" Silas nodded towards the door. "I'll stash her somewhere and let you know. Unless you want her to go to Phoebe?"

Andrew shook his head. "Phoebe won't be home tonight. She's away at a conference the next two days." He sighed. "Can you stay here with her for about an hour? I'll try and be back. If I'm not, I'll send Bill."

Silas nodded. "If we're not here, check the church house."

Andrew paused for a moment, then nodded. "I'll send an unmarked car that way, then."

Silas watched Andrew walk away, then turned back to Aideen.

"How are the feet now?"

"Much better." She reached for the towel. "Thank you, Silas. I didn't realize it would be so far." She sighed, her motions stilling. "Do you think Samuel is okay?"

"I'm sure he is, Aideen. Andrew's working on trying to find him."

❧❧❧

Rousing late the next morning, Aideen raised her head, staring around her. She blinked, trying to remember what had happened. As she swung her feet over the edge of the bed, she grimaced, staring down at the bandages wrapped around them, memory coming back to her as she studied her feet.

Samuel! Where is he, Lord? Please let him be all right.

She dressed, then hesitantly opened the door, not quite sure who or what she'd find on the other side. She headed in what she hoped would be the way to the kitchen. She stopped, not seeing anyone around. She

154

spun, ready to start searching when she heard a voice behind her.

"Good morning, Aideen."

She turned, her eyes narrowing as she stared at the woman standing there.

"I'm sorry. I don't think I know you."

The woman laughed. "No, I don't think we've met. I'm Lily, one of the detectives here in town. Andrew asked me to stay with you for now. He seems to think you need a friend as well as a guardian." Her face lit up with her grin. "Now, tell me, is that true?"

Aideen shook her head. "I'm not sure on that guardian part, but I could use a friend." She moved into the kitchen. "Did he leave any food for us? I don't think I've eaten properly in the last three weeks."

"No, I don't think you have. There's juice in the fridge, I just made coffee, or there's teabags in the cupboard. Quite a selection, I must say. There's bread for toast, eggs, or some frozen stuff." She made a face as she said that.

"Toast is good. I can get it."

"No, stay off your feet. Andrew's worried about them."

"Any word on Samuel?" Aideen's face was hopeful.

"Not that I've heard." She smiled at the downcast look on Aideen's face. "Don't worry. Our guys are great. They'll find him."

"I'm sure they will. I just don't know what they want from me. I don't know anything." Aideen stared at her plate, her mind racing. "I need to be doing something." She rose, walking from the room, to the window in the living room. Lily paused in the doorway.

"What do you think you should be doing, Aideen?"

Aideen shrugged. "There has to be something I can do." She stopped, stepping back from the window. "Lily. Come here. Those men aren't police officers, are they?"

Lily stood behind Aideen. "No, they're not. Come on. We're out of here. The back yard was clear just a moment ago. We should be able to get away. Where are your shoes?"

Aideen paused, then shook her head. "I'm not running, Lily. Besides, how would they know I was here? Silas says he comes and goes from here all the time. It was dark when we came in through the garage."

"That's true. Let's just watch for a moment." The two women stood, hidden from views. The men seemed to be looking at the house across the street from them, finally moving away.

Aideen breathed a sigh of relief. "Let me finish my breakfast. Then I need to find something to do."

"No, you are to stay in this house, Aideen, until Andrew calls. He's working on a new place for us."

Aideen shook her head. "I can't put anyone else at risk." She jumped as she heard a knock at the back door.

Hand on her weapon, Lily headed that way, then opened the door. A tall, younger man entered, his keen eyes on first Lily, then Aideen.

"Richard. I didn't know Andrew had called you." She turned to Aideen. "This is

Richard. He has a security team, and it appears that Andrew has called him in."

"Why?" Aideen didn't know the man and wasn't sure she wanted to complicate her life by adding any new people into it.

"Why what? Why call me?" Richard pulled out a chair, accepting the cup of coffee Lily handed him. "He's worried about you, Aideen, and he doesn't have the officers to put with you that you need right now. My team's free for the next couple of weeks, and if this goes longer than that, I have another friend who'll step in."

"I want this over yesterday." Her disgruntled comment made Richard laugh, drawing her eyes to him.

"I know you do. We'll work on that, okay? But first, we need to do some planning. Just so you know, I'm the team leader. I have two men and two ladies on my team. That's likely why Andrew reached out. Lily here can't stay with you for long. She's needed at the department to work on her cases."

Aideen nodded, then sighed. "So, what's the plan?"

Richard shook his head as he shared a glance with Lily. He had protected many persons over the years, and he didn't think he had seen someone so defeated as Aideen.

Chapter 13

*A*ideen turned from the window she had been staring out and walked back through the house. She knew Richard and his team were around, but she hadn't seen them in the last couple of hours. Lily had headed out, promising to keep in touch. She sighed. She wanted this over, to go back to whatever life she could scrape together. She finally stopped pacing and dropped to the couch, her knees drawn up and her arms wrapped around her legs. She still hadn't gotten it all figured out yet.

Richard watched from the doorway, knowing Aideen hadn't heard him come in. He had just spent time with Andrew and knew what they were facing. Bill had been busy, tracking down the men they thought were involved and trying to trace the plate number Aideen had given them. Both were dead ends, he thought, then frowned. Not quite the way he should have thought that.

He prayed that Samuel was still alive. He didn't know how Aideen would take it, if Samuel wasn't.

Aideen looked up as Richard sank into a chair across from her, her eyes shaded, fatigue lining her face.

"What's the plan, Richard?"

Richard sighed, knowing she wouldn't like it. "We plan to move you out after dark to an unspecified location. Andrew doesn't even know where it will be."

"How safe?"

Richard shrugged. "As safe as any I would say. We don't know who those men were last night, Aideen. Bill's still working on that. Other than that fact, Andrew still doesn't have much to go on."

She laid her head back, her eyes sliding closed. "I should never have come here. I did this." She raised her head. "Barnabas?"

"He knows. He's tied up in a court case but will be back as soon as he can." Richard watched for a moment. "Now, do you need anything? Lily seemed to think you did."

She nodded. "I do, but I can't go shopping, can I?"

He shook his head. "Provide me with a list, and I'll have Silver go. She loves to shop and finds bargains like no one else I know."

Aideen nodded, then rose. "I'll give you a list. I don't need a lot."

"Make sure you have enough for at least two weeks, Aideen." Richard stood as well, staring down at her. "Where we're going, you won't be able to have someone run out to the store for you. And yes, there will be laundry facilities."

She shook her head, as she passed him. "I didn't ask that, Richard."

He sighed to himself. Lord, how do I reach her? She's so withdrawn. He turned and walked to the door, heading out to look for Silver. Stephen approached as he did, his eyes searching for Aideen, watching as she stopped in the kitchen doorway and just stood.

"How is she?"

Richard turned to glance behind him. "I really don't know, Stephen. She's withdrawn, and there's this huge wall she's put up. I don't think we've ever had anyone do that to us."

"No, I don't think we have. Has Andrew said much about her?"

"Not really, other than the basics that we need to know. I'll ask him for more information. It's going to be hard to protect her if we don't know." He turned to look around. "All set at the house?"

"It is. We'll be able to head that way as soon as it's dark."

Richard nodded, as he turned once more to stare through the front door of the house. He watched as Aideen finally moved to the kitchen and then returned to hand him a paper. He thanked her, wondering just how he could reach her.

Lord, you've placed us here. I have no idea why or what we're to do. I don't know enough about her to keep her safe. But You do. Guide us in this. I get the sense she's really struggling right now. Help her to trust. Renew her faith, if that's what is needed.

❧❧❧

Aideen looked around the larger home Richard had brought her to. She couldn't understand how such a beautiful home could be a safe house. It was large, two-storied, and she thought likely decorated by a professional. She stood in the bedroom doorway of the room she had been assigned. Silver stood and watched her.

"It's okay, Aideen. This is the safest room for you."

Aideen nodded before crossing the threshold. Silver followed, dropping the bag she had been carrying near the closet. She walked across to open a door, giving Aideen a glimpse of a large bathroom.

"Why this house, Silver?"

Silver grinned. "Impressive, isn't it? It also has a great security system, cameras around the perimeter, and is fenced. That's why Richard chose it"

"But if I'm here, how do we get Samuel back? Won't they be looking for me in town?"

"They will be. Barnabas will be watching both houses and Samuel's office when he's back. In the meantime, Andrew has one of his officer checking them out, to make sure we don't miss any communications from Samuel's kidnappers."

Aideen gave a weary sigh and sank down onto the bed. "I should eat, but I don't think I can."

"Then sleep. You can eat in the morning. Or if you're up in the night, come find the kitchen. Just so you know, two of us will be on duty at all times. Richard will have some rules he'll go over with you in the morning."

Aideen groaned. "Not more rules. I've had enough of them."

Silver gave a low laugh. "These are meant to keep you alive. Richard's fair with what he wants you to do. You just need to trust him. He's a good guy."

Aideen nodded as she sank down on the bed, her eyes closing in sleep before Silver had left the room. Silver softly closed the door and headed to find Richard,

Richard turned as he heard Silver coming down the stairs, his eyes tracing to the rooms above.

"Aideen get settled in?"

Silver shook her head. "She was asleep before she could. Richard, what's her story?"

Richard shrugged. "I don't rightly know, Silver. Andrew hasn't said, and that's not like him. He usually tells me enough that it makes it easier to keep our protectees safe."

"That is strange. Any word on Samuel?"

Richard shook his head again as he headed for the office he had set up. "No, and that's concerning me. We should have heard something from them by now."

"That is strange. Listen, I'm going to head up to the room next to Aideen. Call me if you need me. And get some sleep yourself, Boss."

Richard grinned at her. That was a standard comment from his team. He didn't sleep a lot when they were on duty. His attention going to his phone as it chimed, he pulled it out. Andrew. Just the person he wants to speak with.

Richard sat back with a sigh after he finished his call with Andrew. He hadn't liked what he had heard from Andrew. He rose, stretched, then went to find Stephen.

"Stephen? I need to talk with you and Timothy and Naomi. Silver's upstairs with Aideen." His three team members approached. "I just got off the phone with Andrew. We have a huge problem."

"I don't like to hear that, Richard." Stephen jammed his hands into his pockets. "What did he have to say?"

"He, or rather Bill, has tracked down one of the men and have him under surveillance. He's from the building department Aideen used to work in."

A sound behind him had him turning and he groaned to himself. Aideen stood here, her eyes watchful.

"Who, Richard? Which one?"

"Dennis."

She repeated the name. "There was no Dennis there when I worked there. I would have remembered. I knew all their names from the reports I read. Why would Bill think that?"

"Trust me, Aideen. He's an employee there. He just wasn't seen around the office. I'm sure there are many more like that."

She stared at him. "So, where does that leave us?"

"It leaves us here. Let Bill do the investigating."

Aideen shook her head as she walked away. "Not happening, Richard. I need to do something." She stopped at the back door, staring out into the predawn darkness. Then before they could reach her, she was out the door and gone.

Richard and Stephen ran for the back door as Naomi and Timothy ran for the front. Silver hesitated, not quite sure where Aideen would have gone but knowing one of the team had to wait in the house. She was frustrated. Why had Aideen ran?

Richard was angry as he returned to the house. He hadn't found Aideen, nor had Timothy or Naomi. Stephen was still looking. He had had a chance to scour the house and outbuildings and had a good idea Aideen was hiding somewhere there. Now, if he could only find her.

A slight noise to his left caused him to turn, his flashlight reflecting off something. He walked forward, seeing Aideen standing there, still as a statue, her eyes staring behind him. Before he could move, a blow to the head had him dropping to his knees, the flashlight rolling away from him. He heard a whimper from Aideen and then blackness overcame him.

Richard walked back outside, Timothy at his side.

"Where are they, Richard?"

"I have no idea. I hope safe." He pointed. "There's light coming from over under that tree." They walked towards it, hands on their weapons.

Timothy bent and picked up the flashlight and shone it around.

"They were here, Richard, but so was someone else. Now what?"

Richard stared at the ground, then pulled out his phone. "Andrew won't be happy, I can tell you that. See if you can find a trail."

Timothy nodded and moved away, his eyes searching for the smallest clue, any

clue. Lord, I know you're in control. You'll
have to lead us in this.

Andrew stood in the yard, staring
around as he listened to Richard.

"I thought no one knew about this
place."

"So do I, Andrew. It's not one we use
a lot. It's not connected to any of us, so how
did they find us? We checked the vehicles
for trackers."

"Aideen doesn't have a phone?"

Richard shook his head. "No, she
doesn't. So how?"

They turned as Silver approached
them. "I think I know how they found us,
Richard." She held out her hand. "I found
this in Aideen's old sneaker. A tracking
device."

"And we searched them, didn't we?"

She nodded. "So where are they?"

❧❧❧

Aideen sat huddled into a corner as
Stephen searched the apartment they had
been taken to. She had fought hard to
escape before Stephen had followed her out

170

of the house, but to no avail. They had been outnumbered. Led to a car, and blindfolded as they left the safe house, Aideen was not sure where they were, but she knew the apartment wasn't in a building in town. She could tell that from the windows.

"Aideen?" She looked up as Stephen crouched down in front of her. "Are you okay?"

She shook her head. "What happened, Stephen? How did they find us?"

"I'm not sure, Aideen. They shouldn't have."

"Where's Samuel? If they have me, won't they release him?"

He nodded. "They might, but somehow I don't think this group is the same as that group. It's almost as if there are two groups working against one another."

She sighed, her head going back against the wall. "Aren't you just a bundle of good news! How do we get out of here?"

"I don't know, Aideen. I'm sure there's someone watching the door. We're on the main floor, so I'm going back to check out the windows again. Maybe we can get away. If anything, I'll make sure you get away."

"I'm not leaving without you, Stephen." She stood, pacing the room.

"If I tell you to run, I expect you to do just that, Aideen. It's more important that you escape."

She sighed again, her eyes turning back to read his face before she finally nodded. "All right. Let's see how we can get out of here."

"I'll work on that. You see if there's anything here that would tell us who they are. First though, give me a hand. We'll move the couch over in front of the door. That will slow them down."

Aideen stared at him, then spun and hurried to the kitchen, returning with some knifes.

"If we stick these against the door and under the trim, it will help slow them down some. Or it should."

Stephen stared at the knives and then at her. "Really?"

She nodded. "I used to stick them into my house door. It helps."

"Some day, I want you to tell me why you had to do that. Now, you search and I'll work on getting us out of here."

Chapter 14

Rolling over onto his back, Samuel ran his hand down his face, wincing as he hit a sore spot. His head still foggy, he cracked his eyes open, trying to focus. He sighed. It was the same way he had found himself yesterday and the day before. He wasn't sure how many days it had been so far. He had been unconscious for most of them. His mouth felt like it was stuffed with dry cotton. He finally managed to push himself up against a wall and sat, his knees raised, forearms resting on them.

Head hanging down, he waited for the fog to clear. He finally raised his head, eyes searching the room he was in. But where was it? He wasn't sure anymore exactly where he was. Lord, I need help. I need to get out of here, wherever here is.

He finally rose to his feet, his hand against the wall to balance him. He searched the room, finding little in it. He shook his head and regretted it, the pain pulsing at his temples. He reached for the window frame, clutching it as he tried to keep upright and balanced. He stared through the glass, seeing trees and then a lake. Where was he? Lord, I have no idea where I am or who has me. I just pray that Aideen is fine.

He stood even as he heard the lock open and the door creak behind him. He didn't care any more what they did to him. Soft footsteps approached and stopped behind him.

"Samuel?" The voice was quiet and familiar.

"Andrew?" Samuel went to turn and then, eyes rolling upwards, he collapsed before Andrew could catch him.

Andrew knelt and felt for a pulse, then called for the paramedics. He stood watching as Ezra and his partner worked on Samuel, before turning to walk from the room.

"Bill, what do we have?"

"Andrew? Not a lot unfortunately. The team says there's not a lot of trace evidence. We figure they dumped Samuel here when they found out Aideen disappeared. You were right. We have two groups working in this."

Andrew made a face, then frowned. "But who are the two groups? That's what I want to know. We know one is connected to her last employer, but how does that connect to here?"

"Bill? Andrew? I think you two need to see this." Ezra stood in the doorway, looking back at Samuel.

"What do we need to see, Ezra?"

Ezra pointed at Samuel. "Someone taped a message to the inside of his shirt. You need to read it."

The two officers shared a glance, before Andrew reached for the note. His mouth tightened as he read it.

"We weren't supposed to find him yet, were we?" He looked down at Samuel, then at Ezra. "How is he?"

"He's been drugged, Andrew, and a fairly high dose I would say. We're ready to roll with him."

"I'll have a patrol car follow you. Bill, we need to process that letter and see what we can find." He read it again.

"Too bad it's too little, too late. You should have cooperated with us, Aideen."

Bill spun to follow Samuel. "I'm riding with him, Andrew. I'll stay until he can talk."

Andrew nodded, knowing nothing would stop Bill, even a direct order not to go. He sighed. They really weren't that much further ahead, except they had Samuel back. Now to find Aideen.

🐾🐾🐾

Barnabas was almost on a run as he hit the entrance to the hospital, searching for someone who could tell him where Samuel was. He had just flown in from his trip and had headed to hospital as soon as he had received Andrew's call. Lily was waiting for him, Andrew having made sure someone would meet him. She pointed to the elevator.

"How is he, Lily?" Barnabas punched the floor button, then stuffed his hands into his pockets to try and stop their shaking.

"He's sleeping, I think, Barnabas. I know he was on his feet when Andrew found him, but he collapsed."

"Collapsed?" Barnabas' eyes were hard. "Did they hurt him?"

Lily shook her head. "I don't know all the details. You'll have to ask Andrew or Bill."

She pointed to Samuel's room. "In there. I'll be out here in the waiting room if you need anything."

Barnabas nodded as he walked quickly towards the room, his runners scuffing softly on the floor. He nodded at the officer standing at the door, then paused to draw in a big breath and attempt at controlling his emotions. Samuel was all he had left now. His wife had died when Samuel was only eight, kidney disease taking her far too soon from them. He pushed at the door, and then paused with his hand on it as his eyes searched the room, flicking across Bill standing at the window before coming to a rest on the bed.

He walked forward, his footsteps soft, until he reached the side of the bed. He winced at the bruising he could see on his son's face, before he looked up at the IV hanging on the pole and then the monitors. He frowned as he realized one was a heart monitor.

"Barnabas?" Bill's voice was quiet as he approached the older man.

"Bill? What did they do to him?"

Bill shook his head. "We don't know exactly, other than he was kept sedated. The staff here are working to determine what exactly it was. They're monitoring his heart just to ensure there's no damage done."

"His heart?" Barnabas blew out a breath as he studied his son. "When did you find him?"

"Late last night, so about twelve hours ago." Bill turned as he heard the door open and a nurse entered. He stepped away from the bed.

Barnabas watched as she took the readings she needed before he spoke.

"What's the news on his waking up?"

She shook her head. "I'm sorry. We really don't know. We need to determine what he was drugged with, then find a medication to counteract it."

"And if you don't?" Barnabas was pushing for answers.

"Then, we wait for it to come out of his system. His physician will be around later this morning."

Barnabas nodded as she excused herself and walked away. He turned once more to his son, tracing the likeness of Samuel's mother in his face.

Please, Lord, don't let me lose him too. I don't know if I could take that.

Barnabas dragged a chair over near the bed and sank into it, his hands scrubbing at his face. He had hated to have been out of town while this was going on but as an expert witness, he had had to be in court. Then a thought crossed his mind.

"Bill, who took him?"

Bill shrugged. "We think the ones after Aideen, but we're not one hundred per cent sure. The note they left indicates that."

"Note?" Barnabas raised his eyes to Bill, their look hardening as he took in the ramifications of what Bill had just said.

Bill nodded. "There was a note with Samuel. It just indicated that Aideen should have done what they wanted."

"And we have no idea what they wanted, now do we?"

Bill shook his head. "We don't. We're getting close to figuring it out. It has something to do with work done here in Elmton. I still haven't connected Aideen to that. Her family weren't part of it."

Barnabas nodded, then looked around. "Where's Aideen? She's tucked away somewhere safe?"

Bill sighed and didn't reply. Barnabas shot him another look, then shook his head.

"No, don't tell me."

"She was taken sometime early yesterday morning. Stephen from Richard's team as well."

"Stephen? How on earth did they get to her?"

"That we don't know yet. Richard's working on that as well. Apparently, Aideen had a tracking device in her sneaker. That's how she was found."

"It just doesn't stop, now does it, Bill?" Barnabas sat back, his eyes on his son as Samuel moved restlessly. His eyes narrowed as he watched, then reached to touch Samuel's face.

"Bill, can you take a look at this? There's something in that bruise?"

Bill came closer and studied it. "You're right. It looks like it's from a ring, doesn't it?" Bill pulled out his phone and took a photo of the mark, sending it off to the lab. "I'll have one of the tech work on that. Now, how did we miss that?"

"Because you weren't looking for it, I would guess." Barnabas sat back, his eyes still on Samuel. "You don't have to stick around, Bill, if you need to be elsewhere."

Bill shrugged. "I can stay, but I should head into the office."

"Then, go. Keep me updated on the investigation, please."

Bill watched for a moment, before he moved away, the door swishing closed behind him. Barnabas sat back, his head burrowed in his hands as he prayed. A soft movement raised his head. Samuel's eyes were blinking as he tried to focus.

Rising, Barnabas approached the beside, his hand on his son's arm.

"Samuel?"

Samuel's head turned, as he frowned, trying to focus.

"Dad?"

"Right here, son."

Samuel had trouble swallowing and speaking and Barnabas reached for the glass and helped him to drink.

"Can you raise my head, Dad?" Once he sitting up, he looked around, still trying to properly focus. "Where am I?"

"In the hospital. Samuel, can you remember anything?"

Samuel shook his head. "No, really. Everything is just so foggy. What did they do to me?"

"Drugged you by what I'm told."

"What day is it?"

"Thursday."

Samuel finally nodded. "Almost a week then?" His head went back against the pillow. "I don't know why they took me. I can sort of remember hearing them talk, but I can't remember rightly what they were saying."

"Don't try, then. God will let you remember when you need to ."

Samuel nodded, then looked around, his head turning to watch the monitors. "A heart monitor?"

"They need to make sure whatever you were given hasn't caused any heart issues."

"When can I leave?"

Barnabas barked out a laugh. "Not today, that's for certain. You'll be back asleep before long, son."

Samuel nodded once more, his eyes on his father. "What aren't you telling me, Dad? Where's Aideen?"

"That we don't know, Samuel. I don't know all the details but she showed up at the church, Silas called Andrew, who called Richard. She was in Richard's safekeeping but someone somehow got to her. She's disappeared as has Stephen."

Samuel's head went back on the pillow again as his eyes slid shut. Barnabas watched as a tear trickled out from under the closed eyelids.

"They're trying to find her, son. Andrew and Bill think there are two different groups involved."

"Two different groups. Which is the more dangerous?" Samuel straightened up, reaching to pull the IV from his arm and the heart monitor leads from his chest. "Find my clothes, Dad. I'm out of here." He staggered as he stood, his father reaching to steady him as a nurse shoved open the door and headed into the room.

"What's going on here?" She stared at Samuel, then went to turn off the monitor. "You can't leave yet."

Samuel stared her down. "I can and I will. Find the physician to get my release papers. If you don't I'm still leaving."

"Think it through better, son. You're no good to Aideen with you in the shape you are now. Stay until tomorrow morning at least."

Samuel sank back to a sitting position on the bed, nodding, knowing his father was right. "Until tomorrow morning. Then I'm gone. But no more monitors or IV's."

The nurse shook her head. "I can't make that determination, Samuel. It has to be your physician that does that. For now, the monitor goes back on and the IV goes back in."

❧❧❧

Stephen struggled with the window at the back of the house, finally seeing the screws holding it in place. He studied it, only seeing the one.

"Aideen, did you happen to see something we could use as a screwdriver?"

She shook her head, then headed back to the kitchen drawer, quickly looking through it.

"Just a knife, Stephen, or a spoon. Would that work?"

"It might." He took it from her.

She watched for a moment, then reached beside him to grasp at the window. "This window should lift right up. I had some like it in my apartment. I would take them out to clean them."

Stephen watched her for a moment, then reached for the window. It shifted in his hand. "I think if we can get one side up, we can use the knife running along under it to raise it enough to get it out. Watch yourself."

Aideen stood back for a moment and watched as Stephen worked away at the window, finally freeing the window from the track and lifting it out. He turned to study the door, hearing nothing. He turned back and reached for the screen, pausing to study the area outside.

"Here, let me out first, and then I'll reach back for you. Did you find anything that would help identify them?"

She nodded. "I might have. I have it tucked away somewhere safe."

He shook his head. "That I'm glad of. Here goes."

Stephen disappeared through the window, then reached up to help her down. He crept to the edge of the house, listening and then peeking around the corner. Finger first to his mouth in a quietening movement, he pointed towards the garage.

They ran quickly for the building, ducking behind it as they reached it. Stephen led Aideen along the back of it, not daring to enter it yet. He peeked into a window, then back at Aideen. He motioned towards the door at the back. She nodded and followed him inside. He looked around. The only vehicle was a dirt bike. He approached it, studying it. He had raced dirt bikes as a teenager. Checking it for fuel, he looked around for a gas can. Finding one that was full, he filled the tank, then wheeled the bike to the door they had entered through. He searched once more and found two helmets, handing one to Aideen.

Wheeling the bike out, he headed for the back of the yard, eyes watchful, Aideen close behind him. It was starting to darken, night falling slowing.

"We'll walk a ways yet, Aideen. These bikes are noisy when they start. As soon as I think it's safe, we'll be off. They won't be able to follow us where I'll head."

She nodded, then hesitated. "Stephen, did God just do this?"

"Do what, Aideen?" He stopped, his eyes on her face, knowing what she was asking but wanting her to verbalize ie.

"Did He just get us out of there, provide transportation, and let us walk away from them?" She pointed back over her shoulder.

Stephen nodded. "He did, Aideen. It's what He can and will do. He knew we would be there. He gave you the knowledge about the windows. He had a dirt bike left in the garage for us. He helped us walk away without being seen. So, yeah, I guess you can say, He did it."

"So, is this where trust and faith come in?" She was struggling, she knew, trying to understand how God would take care of a measly human being, as that was how she saw herself.

"He loves you, Aideen. He loved you before you were even born. So He planned this for you all those years ago. He put you in situations where you gained knowledge of what to do. Just as He let me race dirt bikes as a teenager. That knowledge is going to get us out of here.”

She nodded, then sighed. “What have I missed, Stephen, all these years? I’ve been trusting in myself, not God. Maybe I wouldn’t be in this situation if I had trusted God more.”

Stephen shook his head as he started moving again. “I think you still would have been. God is using you to bring some people to justice. You’re the one He’s chosen to use. We never know what God plans for us. I have a friend, Murphy, on another security team. His favourite saying is that God has a plan and purpose for us and we don’t know what it is. He’ll then add we just need to trust God.”

“Okay, I get that. But who are these guys?” She stopped, causing Stephen to stop as well. She pulled a paper from her jeans’ pocket. “This is what I found. What does it mean, Stephen?”

Stephen reached for it, studying her as he did so, a prayer in his heart for God to help him get her out of there. "What is it, Aideen?"

"It's a bank statement of some kind, Stephen. I don't recognize the name."

Stephen read the name and sighed. Yes, he thought, it's two different groups, but with one leader. "This is what Andrew will need to solve this. Here, stick it back into your pocket." She didn't take it. "Put it back in your pocket, Aideen. Fold it as small as you can. They won't search you if they find us again, but they will me."

She whitened at the thought of being found again, finally taking the paper and doing what Stephen asked.

"Do you have any idea where we are?"

Stephen nodded. "I do. I used to ride through here with my Dad and brother. We're about ten miles from Elmton. I know where we can find someone to help us." He swung his leg over the bike. "Hop on. It's a tight fit, but we should be fine. It's not that far where I'm thinking to go."

❧❧❧❧

Samuel walked into his father's kitchen the next morning and sank gratefully into a chair. Against his physician's wishes, he had insisted he be discharged. They still hadn't identified exactly what he had been drugged with but the feeling was it had been a sedative of some kind. All he knew what that he was exhausted and drained.

"Do you want anything to eat, son?" Barnabas moved to make them coffee.

"Maybe just some toast, Dad. Any word on Aideen?"

Barnabas shook his head. "Not yet. Andrew finally had to send Bill home with orders not to come near the office for a day. He's been there 24/7 since this started."

Samuel nodded, then laid his head down on his folded arms. "Why? Why did this happen, Dad?"

Barnabas leaned back against the counter, his arms folded across his chest.

"I don't rightly know, son, but I know God does. He's in control, whether or not it feels like it."

He looked over towards the door as a tap came, and then Silas entered. He nodded. Somehow Silas always knew when he was needed most.

"Morning, Silas. Here for breakfast, are you?"

Silas laughed. "I never turn down the offer of food, you know me. I'll take a cup of your coffee as well."

Barnabas laughed as he shook his head.

"What brings you by?"

Silas sat, his eyes on Samuel. "I was hoping you could tell me that, Samuel."

Samuel's head raised and a frown covered his face. "Me? How?"

Silas just stared at him. "I had the strongest impression I needed to be here, with you, right now, right here. So, you tell me, why?"

Barnabas watched as Samuel struggled to make sense of it. Samuel finally shrugged.

"I have no idea, Silas. I really don't."

Silas nodded. "That's sometimes how it works. I'm told to show up, not knowing why, and the other person has no idea why either. God works it all out." He nodded his thanks as Barnabas handed him a plate of food. "Now, tell me, any word on Aideen?"

Samuel shook his head. "I have no idea. Andrew didn't tell me, but he might have said something to Dad."

Barnabas shook his head. "No one's said anything to me." His head turned as he heard a noise from the back of the yard, and he walked towards the door, his posture freezing for a moment before he reached for the door.

Silas stood, nodding. This is why God had put him there. Aideen walked in, followed by Stephen.

Samuel spun in his chair, his vision momentarily blurring. He rose, walked towards Aideen and stopped.

"You're here!" He reached and pulled her into a hug.

Tears sparkled on her face as she buried it against him.

Silas stared at them, then at Stephen, finally reaching to direct Stephen to a chair and shoving a cup of coffee in front of him. Barnabas stood for a moment, then locked the door, heading to close the drapes and blinds, before pulling out his phone.

"Andrew? They're here. They just walked in the door."

"Aideen? Stephen?" To say Andrew was shocked would be a mild statement. "Just walked in?"

"They did. They haven't said anything. How about you and Phoebe dropping in for breakfast? I have lots."

"We'll do that. We're on our way."

Chapter 15

Andrew and Phoebe walked into the house ten minutes later, Phoebe heading right for Aideen and pulling her away from the kitchen.

"Aideen, come with me." Phoebe headed for the bedroom Aideen had been using. "We need to get you cleaned up, you know."

Aideen nodded, her exhaustion beginning to show. She grabbed the clothes she was handed and headed for a shower, her mind trying to figure out who and why.

Phoebe turned as Aideen came back into the bedroom, fatigue evident in the slowness of her moves.

"Why don't you lie down for a while, Aideen? We're not going anywhere."

Aideen nodded. "I will. But I need to give Andrew this." She held up the folded piece of paper she had tucked into her jeans' pocket. "I found it in the house we were held in."

Phoebe looked past her as Andrew appeared in the doorway. "Andrew's right here, Aideen. Tell him the basics and then go to bed."

Andrew listened without questions as Aideen told him what had happened. He unfolded the paper, his hand stilling as he read the name.

"This was in the apartment? They got careless, Aideen, or rather, someone did. We'll look into it. Now, I think you need to do what Phoebe has suggested. You're not hurt in any way? No? Need anything to eat or drink? No? Okay, you sleep. We'll be here when you wake up."

Andrew and Phoebe watched as Aideen sank down onto the bed, not even bothering to pull a cover over herself. Phoebe reached for the blanket folded up on the chair and covered her new friend before turning to Andrew. Andrew closed the door behind them as they headed for the kitchen.

Samuel sat up, more alert than he had been and watched behind the couple.

"Aideen's asleep, Samuel." Andrew watched with concern the looks crossing his friend's face.

Samuel nodded. "She needs it, likely. I doubt she's slept much in the last few months."

Andrew stood leaning against the counter, coffee cup in hand, his eyes searching first Stephen and then Samuel.

"Okay, Samuel. You first. Have you remembered anything?"

He shook his head, fatigue clouding his brain. "I can't think of anything, Andrew. The last I remember was walking up to my door and then nothing. I have vague bits and pieces but not clear enough to mean anything." He looked up, his eyes shuttered. "Who did this to us, Andrew? Please tell me you know."

"We're working on it, Samuel. Stephen, how about you? We do need to get a statement from both you and Aideen."

Stephen nodded, pausing to sip his coffee, and then take a bite of food as he gathered his thoughts.

"We were in a home about 10 miles from here. I don't remember much about how we got there. I can remember seeing Aideen standing outside the safe house, not saying anything. I think there was someone standing behind her. I woke up in the car, blindfolded.   We were dumped in that apartment and then left there.   Strangest thing.   They didn't remove any of the utensils that we could use for a weapon. I think there was someone outside the front door, but I can't be positive. Aideen found that paper there, Andrew.

"We were there for about a day, I think. No one came near us. You'll need to watch her, Barnabas. We had no food the whole time we were there."

Stephen paused at this point and laughed, drawing a frown from Samuel. "Sorry, Samuel.   What Aideen did was priceless. We moved the couch in front of the door to slow them down if they decided to come back in. Aideen disappeared and returned with knives. Yep, just like these and insisted on sticking them under the trim. She was adamant they would slow down whoever was trying to get in. She also had the idea of how to get the window out. It was locked in place with a screw through the track. She apparently has had experience with these types of windows and knew how to get them out. Once we were out and sure no one was around, we headed for the garage, found a dirt bike, walked out until I thought it was safe to ride, and then headed for a neighbour's house."

"How'd you know it was safe?" Barnabas was still trying to take in what Stephen had said.

Stephen looked up at him. "I used to ride out there a lot with my Dad and brother. Dad was friends with the man who lived about three miles from that house. Andrew, it's worth your while to talk to him. He has some information you'll need."

Andrew nodded, his notebook in hand to jot down what Stephen had been saying. "We'll need you to come down and make a formal statement, Stephen. I spoke with Richard. He'll be here this afternoon." He paused, not quite sure how to continue. Lord, I need the words to say what I have to say and I'm not sure I have them.

"Stephen, Samuel. From what we can gather, you each taken by an opposing group. But this statement? This person we never looked at. I would hazard a guess to say he's in charge of both, just from what you've said, Stephen. Why they took you and Aideen, I have no idea. It doesn't sound like they really thought through how to keep you captive."

Stephen sat back, eyes on Andrew, finally pointing a finger at him. "That's what I don't get. Silver found a tracking device in one of Aideen's old runners. That's how the safe house was found. But why did they take her? You didn't get a ransom note, a letter demanding anything, did you?" When Andrew shook his head, Stephen continued. "It was just too bizarre. I know it was out in the country and they made some attempt at keeping us out there, but it was like they wanted us to find a way out and back here."

Andrew nodded as he caught a look on Barnabas' face. "I think you're right, Stephen. They wanted you to come back. But why?"

Barnabas stood, heading for the counter to refill his coffee cup. "That name you have there, Andrew? I know him. I've always suspected he's been involved in crime, just skirting along the edge. He's also a distant relative of Aideen's, the wrong side of the family, shall we say? It's beginning to make sense to me. I have some more research to do on that, thought, before I can give you everything I have."

"Don't let it be too long, Barnabas. We need to end this now." Andrew looked as Silas, who nodded. "Silas, can you stay for a while? Phoebe's staying as well. I need to head for the office and find Lily and Bill." He walked out the door, leaving the group in the kitchen staring at one another.

"Stephen, Samuel. Go find somewhere to sleep for a while. Stephen, there's a bedroom down stairs you can use. You two need to catch up on some sleep. We'll talk more this afternoon." Barnabas pointed at the two men.

Phoebe reached to start clearing the table as the two men walked away, but stopped when Barnabas' hand was laid on her arm.

"Phoebe, you're thinking hard. What about?"

She nodded, seeing Samuel had stopped in the doorway and was looking back. "I just had a thought, Barnabas, as to why Stephen and Aideen were taken. It wasn't to keep them safe. It wasn't to put them in harm. It was to send a message to the other group, that this group could and would walk in and take over." She looked up, fear in her eyes. "What have they walked into?"

Samuel approached her. "Why do you say that, Phoebe?"

She shrugged. "I don't know, Samuel. It's just an impression I had."

Samuel stared at her. "There must be something more than that, Phoebe. Talk to us." He sat, not intending on moving until she did.

She turned to watch him. "Why were you taken, Samuel? Was it to get Aideen to come out into the open so that they could take her? More than likely that's the reason. But why was Aideen and Stephen taken? They didn't question them. They just took them and dumped them into a house. I would suggest there was never a guard at the front door, but they couldn't take a chance on them getting away. Why leave a dirt bike there for them to get away on unless they knew Stephen could ride one? I would suggest whoever was behind that abduction knew Richard's team would be called in and they have studied every one of them, just like they've studied each one of Andrew's men and women."

Barnabas stilled in his movements of clearing the kitchen. "Do you realize what you're suggesting, Phoebe?"

She nodded. "After going through what I did, I suspect I no longer have the trust I once did. I would suggest they've hired a private investigator to research the main players here, including you, Barnabas."

Barnabas stared at her, before his eyes slid shut. "And I know who they'd get. She'll do anything for money. A group of us have been watching her for months, trying to find something to have her charged with and her license revoked. This may well be it." He walked from the room, heading for his office and his contacts.

Samuel shook his head. "It just keeps snowballing, doesn't it? So how do we stop it?"

"I have a suggestion, Samuel." Silas finally spoke up. "We need to get you steady on your feet first thought." Silas outlined his plan, Samuel objecting at first, until Phoebe weighed in and added definition to it.

"Do you really think it will work?" For the first time in weeks, Samuel felt hope.

"It should. Let me work on my part. Your part is to recuperate as fast as you can. I think a week from Saturday should be the right timing. That will give Andrew time to put a plan in place on his part. Your Dad, now we have to keep him out of the loop on this, Samuel. He'll want to take the brunt of it and it won't work if he does."

"I know. But how?"

Chapter 16

The Saturday of the following week found Samuel and Aideen standing in a local park, waiting for Silas to appear. They had set their plan in motion. Aideen wasn't too sure about it, but she had learned to trust the man standing beside her. She had spent time in the Bible and prayer for the last week and could finally say she got what Stephen had told her.

Richard's team was spread out around the perimeter of the park, and she knew Andrew had officers there as well in plains clothes. Samuel gripped her hand and then looked down at her.

"Are you sure about this, Aideen? We can call it off."

She shook her head. "No, I think Silas has come up with a good plan. I just worry about the innocent people who might get hurt. Who would have thought of using a church picnic to draw someone out? Won't the church fire Silas if something happens here and they find out it was his plan?"

"Silas has talked to the church board, and they've agreed we need to do something. Whether you know it or not, you've become part of our church family, Aideen, and they will do just about anything to protect us."

Startled, she looked up at him. "That's not right, Samuel. They don't know me well enough to do that."

"But they know Silas, Dad, me, Andrew. They trust them and have faith that they will do everything to keep our church family safe. We're staying on the edge of the group, just for safety's sake, and we'll have people with us to protect us. They'll be the buffer between the church family and us."

She nodded, still not convinced that this was the right plan. She sighed. This is where trust comes in, isn't it, Lord? How do I trust You to keep us safe? It's not in me to trust someone I can't see or touch. You'll need to show me proof today.

Samuel grasped her hand tight in his as he heard Silas' voice and then turned to face his friend.

Silas stopped, his eyes watchful, taking in the determination in Samuel's face but the hesitation in Aideen's.

"Second thoughts, Aideen?"

She nodded. "I don't want to put these people at risk, Silas."

He nodded. "That's part of the reason this is a young adult only picnic. No children here. We didn't want to risk them."

"Why here, though, Silas? Why this park?" Aideen looked around, not sure of why.

"It's a smaller park, easier to manage for security. Not a lot of places to hide either. We'll notice someone coming who doesn't belong."

Samuel hesitated. "But what if whoever it is belongs to our group? Have we even considered that possibility?"

Silas stared at Samuel for a moment, then shook his finger at him. "Don't even suggest that, Samuel. That's the last thing we want to hear, you know that?"

Aideen stopped walking, bringing the two men to a stop as well. "You know, Samuel could be right. What if it's someone in the church? Had you ever considered how he or she know I was staying where I was and that I was working for Samuel? I don't think he or Barnabas told too many people, did you, Samuel?"

He shook his head. "Other than the staff at the town hall and my friends, it was only at church that it was mentioned, and then only to a small group, our Bible study group, Silas." His eyes slid closed. "What have we done, Silas?"

Silas nodded. "I know. I'm beginning to think now this was a bad idea. We have some of that group here." He turned looking for Andrew. "Andrew and Bill are here, are they not?"

Andrew and Phoebe were near them, and the three headed for him. Andrew saw them coming, saw the grim looks on their faces, and sighed. So much for enjoying a picnic with his sweetheart.

"Phoebe, I think our picnic just went south."

"What do you mean?" She looked to where he nodded. "They're looking a little grim, are they not? Was this not a good idea?"

"Andrew, we have a huge problem." Silas' words floated ahead of him.

"And what would that be?"

Silas explained what they had just discovered. Andrew's face hardened.

"Then we get the two of you out of here. Silas, you can't leave."

Silas shook his head. "I can. I'm not really needed here. The board understands what we were up to. It's more important to get these two out of here."

Andrew nodded, then looked around, finding both Bill and Richard walking towards them.

"You're not looking happy, Andrew." Bill studied his chief's face, then the faces of the others. "What did we do now that we shouldn't have?"

"Bring these two here. Samuel's remembered that only a few people knew about Aideen and where she was living and working."

Bill groaned. "We were so busy investigating the other that we totally overlooked that, now didn't we? How'd we do that?"

Andrew shook his head. "We did, and now we have to make plans to get these two safe." He pulled out his phone. "Is your Dad home today, Samuel?"

"He should be. He had some errands this morning, but said he'd be home the rest of the day. He's working on that investigator."

Andrew nodded, then turned to Richard. "Where's your team, Richard?"

"Around here. I can bring them in."

"Do that, please. I have a bad feeling we're not going to get too far without trouble."

Richard nodded as he spoke into his com link. He could see his team approaching them.

"Now what, Andrew? Where do we head?"

"For now, I'd say Barnabas' place. We'll regroup there. Bill, find your team and have them surround the vehicles as we leave. Richard, you have these two in your care. If for some reason we get separated, find a safe place to hunker down and let me know where you are. Phoebe, let Richard have your cell number. We may need to communicate through you until I can get some new phones for these two."

Phoebe nodded, then spoke. "Andrew, why not take them to the old home we bought? No one knows we have it."

Andrew stopped, then turned to study his wife. "That's a thought, love. It has a good security system in it, it's fenced, and Abel has those guard dogs there. Let's regroup first with Barnabas and then go from there."

Samuel held Aideen's hand tightly as they walked towards the SUVs, not wanting to let her go or to let her out of his sight. Lord, help us protect this lady who's begun to mean so much to me. I don't want to lose her.

Tucked inside the vehicles, they waited for Richard and Andrew to finish talking. Andrew's eyes scanned the group left in the park, his gaze stopping at one particular couple, who stood watching them.

He sighed. He may have just found the ones he was looking for. He spoke quietly to Richard, then turned to Phoebe and headed back towards the group, an excuse for Samuel's and Aideen's departure on his lips.

❧❧❧

Samuel paced the living room, his thoughts on what had happened that afternoon. *How long, Lord, do we have to run and hide? I need to get back to my work and it's just not happening.* He turned as he heard footsteps behind him. Stephen and Timothy stood there, watching.

"Samuel? We're going to head out once it's dark. Hopefully we can throw off whoever it is that's behind this." Stephen stopped as he saw the look on Samuel's face. "No, we're not ready to make a stand yet. You tried that this afternoon, being out in the open as targets. Richard and Andrew both don't want that to happen again. Not yet."

"I'm not hiding much longer, Stephen. I want this over so both Aideen and I can go on with our lives."

Stephen started to snicker, drawing Samuel's eyes to him. "You sound like every other friend of yours, including Andrew. All of them said the very same thing at some point or other."

Samuel glared at him, then smiled. "I guess I'm in good company then." He looked past the two men to the kitchen. Richard stood in the doorway watching them.

"What's the news, Richard? You don't look happy."

"I'm not, Samuel. We need to move you two again, and I don't like moving around so much. It causes problems with trying to keep you two safe."

"Where to now?"

Richard shook his head. "You won't know until we're on the road. We're planning on taking you in separate vehicles." He stopped speaking as Samuel shook his head.

"That's not happening, Richard. We go together or we don't go at all."

Richard sighed, having already come to that conclusion. "So, we'll work with that. We're planning on pulling out around midnight. Your Dad's going with us this time around."

"He is? He didn't say that."

"Yeah, he is. I don't like it but he won't have it any other way. He's with Andrew right now, giving him all the information he's been able to come up with. Andrew's hoping to have arrest and search warrants tomorrow or by Monday at the latest."

"But it still won't be over then, will it? Not until you know you have everyone involved arrested?"

Richard nodded. "You'll be kept in hiding for a few days."

Samuel shook his head. "I can't do that, Richard. I have deadlines I'm working on that I need to complete the paperwork on. I can't just walk away from it."

"Then tell us what you need from your office, provide the keys, and I'll have someone pick everything up for you. Do you have a laptop that you use? I would prefer that you use one of ours."

Samuel nodded. "That will work." He reached for a piece of paper. "I'll make a list of everything that I think I'll need. Do you have a laptop Aideen can work on as well? She does a lot of the paperwork for me."

"We can do that." Richard looked at Timothy. "You and Naomi head over there and get what we need."

Aideen stood and watched from the hallway, not quite sure what was going on but knowing in her heart the next two days would change her life completely. She just wasn't sure how. Samuel's eyes found her and she drew strength the from steadiness and determination she saw there. She saw something else as well, something that warmed her heart. She would need to ask him about that at some point, but not right now. Her emotions were all over the place, and as much as she knew now that she loved Samuel, she wasn't sure if she was ready to know he loved her back.

Richard turned at that moment, and he sighed. Another couple in love, Lord. Why do I always end up protecting them?

"Aideen, we'll be moving out around midnight. Pack what you'll need for about four days or so. I'm praying that it's not that long. Samuel has asked us to pick up his work for him. That should keep both of you busy. I would imagine with everything that's been going on, he's quite far behind."

"I likely am, but I have a friend who picked up for me at Dad's request, so it might not be quite as bad as I think it is."

❧❧❧

Under the cover of a cloudy midnight sky, the team left Barnabas' house in two vans. Barnabas was with Timothy and Naomi. Aideen had asked for Silver and Stephen to travel with them. Richard was as well. Aideen sighed, laying her head on Samuel's shoulder, her hand tight in his, as fatigue washed over her. She couldn't remember the last time she had been so tired.

Richard pocketed his phone and turned to watch them. "Andrew's moving on the arrest warrants. He has a judge waiting to sign off on them. As soon as he has them, his teams are moving in."

"Just how many are we looking at?" Samuel really wasn't sure how many were involved.

"Andrew's looking at ten or twelve right now. They're still working through the documents and information they've seized already."

Samuel nodded, his eyes tracing to the darkness outside the vehicle. He had no idea where they were heading, nor did he want to. His hand tightened on Aideen's. He felt her relax against him in sleep. Good, he thought. She needs that.

Richard turned to face the front once again, eyes searching the darkness. He could feel something or someone out there, watching. He knew in all likelihood they had been followed. Stephen was driving in circles at the moment. Timothy was doing the same but in opposite directions from them. He prayed they could keep the two with him safe.

Chapter 17

$\mathscr{R}$ichard breathed a sigh of relief as Stephen pulled into the garage at the safe house. They were here, but for how long and who knew if someone would find them again. Andrew was adamant it was not one of his officers, and Richard believed him. He turned in his seat to study the two behind him as Silver and Stephen headed into the house.

Samuel's head was resting on Aideen's as they both slept. Richard hated to wake them but he knew he had to. He watched as Stephen came back out, nodding that all was well in the house.

He roused the couple sitting in the back seat and sent them into the house. He walked out the side door of the garage to make his own survey of the property. Entering through the front door, he locked it and set the security system before heading to find Stephen and Silver. He knew Timothy was almost there as well.

Samuel sat in the kitchen, staring at the wall. Richard could see no sign of Aideen, fully expecting that.

"Richard, now what?" Samuel's voice was tired.

"Now we wait. We'll get you set up to work tomorrow and hopefully you won't be too far behind on what you've been doing."

Samuel nodded, fully knowing that someone would have to make a trip to the town hall for him as soon as they could.

"I hope not. I'll find out when I dig into it tomorrow. Dad almost here?"

Richard nodded as he sat across from Samuel. "He should be. Timothy was heading in the opposite direction from us." He paused. "Aideen asleep?"

Samuel nodded. "She was heading that way when we came in. If I don't get a chance later, I want to thank you and your team, Richard, for what you've done for us."

Richard nodded. "It's what we do, Samuel. It's just harder when it's friends involved."

It was Samuel's turn to nod. He rose and set his cup in the sink before heading for his bed.

Richard sighed as he watched him walk away. Please, Lord, we need this over with. He pulled out his phone as it ran.

"Andrew?"

"We served the warrants, Richard. Give us a day or so to get everything in order, and then they can all come home." Andrew's voice held fatigue but also a sense of having achieved their goal.

"That's good news, Andrew. I'll tell them the morning."

"All's safe where you are?"

"It is. Timothy's just pulled in, so we're all under one roof now. I know you won't, but try and get some sleep."

Andrew laughed. "I doubt I will for the next twenty-four hours but then I'll take a couple of days."

"Make sure you do. You know first-hand what it's like to be on this side and on that side. Don't wear yourself out."

੬੭੬੭੬੭

Richard watched the next day as Samuel and Aideen worked through the pile of search requests he had accumulated in the last couple of weeks. He realized how well they worked together, each seeming to anticipate what the other was doing or needing.

Silver stopped beside him. "They make quite the team."

"That they do. It's good to see them focused on something other than staying safe." Richard watched as Aideen raised her head to ask Samuel something and then froze in place, her eyes focusing on the paper she held.

"Samuel? Do you have the rest of this search you just gave me?"

"The O'Dell one? I'm just finishing it up. Why?" Samuel's eyes finally raised from the laptop he was working on and he studied her.

"Because I don't think Andrew got everyone. I remember this person's name. It was only in one document, but my boss was very particular that everything was just so in the report. Why? It was for a property just outside Elmton."

Samuel reached for the paperwork Aideen had printed. "You're sure?" When she nodded, he sighed. "This is one of the founding families as well. Dad's always been suspicious of them. They have tons of money, but no real employment. None of them ever did. This could well be connection between the groups."

Richard had walked towards them as they spoke.

"Problems?"

Samuel nodded. "I need to speak with Andrew."

"Let me. Give me the information and I'll get in touch with him. It's better that way. I'll call from here and you can relay anything to me you want to tell him."

Andrew's voice held shock, then determination when Richard had explained what the two had found.

"That makes awful sense, you know. I didn't think we had everyone. We never do, you know. We need to do more digging, I guess."

"Just a minute, Andrew. Barnabas is here." Richard handed Barnabas his phone.

"Andrew? I just walked in on this. Yes, that's the person you need to look at with a fine tooth comb. They've covered up where they get their money from, but from what I've dug up, they're dirty and have been since day one. I know. I don't know how we missed it, but we did."

Andrew sighed. "Can someone bring me that information or at least email it to me for starters? Bill and Lily are here with me. We'll start our search. You know what this means."

Richard sighed as well. "It means we're in a holding pattern here. Don't take too long, okay, friend?"

Samuel looked at Richard, then back at Aideen before reaching for her hand.

"We have to stay safe, Aideen, and here's the best place. Andrew will work fast. If they're that dirty, what Dad has found will help."

She nodded, then shaking off his hand, reached for the paperwork she was finishing off. "We'll need to get all this to the town hall tomorrow, Samuel. They're due by Tuesday at the latest."

He stepped back for a moment, his eyes on her, then sat back at the laptop.

"We do, but we're getting there, Aideen. Dad said he'd take it all in for us."

She nodded once again, her eyes down on the paperwork, but not reading what was in front of her. Her thoughts were racing. Lord, is this where I need to trust you completely? I just don't have that ability but I want to.

She sighed, standing and moving away from the table, heading for the living room. She paced, Silver watching her.

Silver finally approached her. "Aideen, what's up?"

Aideen shot a look back into the dining room where Samuel's head was bent over his work, then to the kitchen where the men had gathered. Naomi she knew was outside.

"I don't know." She shrugged as she said it. "I just have this sense of impending doom. Does that make sense?"

Silver nodded, then pointed to the couch. "Sit, Aideen. Let's talk this through."

Aideen slumped to the couch, her head resting on the back. "I can't explain it properly, Silver. It's just this sense I have that something's about to happen. I've had that all my life, knowing when something was coming up that would dramatically change my life. It usually meant a move to a worse-than-ever foster home." She raised her head, her eyes thoughtful. "I never had that happy home with parents, siblings, that I needed. I've always had to hide away my thoughts, feelings. The only time I didn't was when I was about 16. I was in a foster home with two other teens the same age. The girl didn't care about anything but drugs and living a wild life. The boy. He became a friend. I wish I knew where he was now. He helped so much. He had been raised in a Christian home and lost his parents in a flash flood. He shouldn't have even been in that home but for some reason he was. We finally ran away and took to the streets, feeling that was the only way we could survive. He left one day to find us something to eat but never came back. I don't know what happened to him."

"What was his name?"

"Paul. He said he wanted to be a police officer, but I don't know if he ever made that dream. I lived in a homeless shelter and managed to finish high school. I worked my way through college. Now you tell me, where was God in this?"

"God was there beside you. Did you have any narrow escapes when you were on the street? You managed to achieve what you needed to. God kept you safe and gave you the ability to finish school and go on to college."

Aideen stared thoughtfully at Silver. "I never thought of it that way before, but you're right. What have I done, Silver?"

"What you have done is be human, Aideen. We all go through stages where we doubt and can walk away from God." Silver looked up as Richard stopped in the doorway, his phone in his hand.

Barnabas stood behind him. "This Paul she spoke about? Is that Paul that works for Don?"

Richard nodded. "I think it is. Let me call him and find out. If it is, we'll get them together at some point. But I know one thing, Barnabas, he's just a friend. Your son there has her heart."

Barnabas turned to watch Samuel. "I think you're right. I know she has his. I can see it in the way they react to one another."

❧❧❧

Samuel finally sat back late that evening, confident that he had been able to catch up, thanks to the help of some friends. He stood, stretched, and went looking for Aideen. Not finding her, he headed for the kitchen, finally getting a whiff of the food that had been prepared.

Aideen looked up as he approached, then back down at her plate. She had no appetite even though the food was delicious. She finally stood, walking past Samuel and heading for the room she was using. She just couldn't speak with anyone at the moment.

Samuel watched her walk past him, not saying anything, then turned back to the kitchen, to find his father's eyes on him.

"Dad?"

228

"Sit, son. Have something to eat. Then we'll talk." Barnabas' eyes met Richard's, seeing the relief in his.

"Why, Dad? What do we need to talk about?"

"Eat." Barnabas pushed away his own plate.

Samuel shook his head. "No, I'm not hungry. Tell me what's going on."

Richard moved to sit at the table, just the three of them. "I've heard from Andrew. They arrested Teddy O'Dell. That should be the last one, we're thinking."

"We can go home?" Samuel's voice was hopeful.

"We can. Richard's making arrangements for that to happen tomorrow. They want us under one roof for a few days, just to ensure we're safe. But we can go about our normal life."

Samuel's body slumped with relief. Hands shaking as he reached for his cup, he sipped the coffee. "It's over, then?"

"For all intents and purposes, it is, Samuel. We'll just stay a few days to make sure, but Andrew's confident they've arrested them all.   Aideen's work this morning made that possible."

"Does Aideen know?"

Barnabas nodded. "She does, son, but she's uncertain as to what she wants to do. This is the culmination of a lifelong journey of terror for her. We need to be there for her and pray hard for her."

Samuel studied his father's face. "I know, Dad. I know that. I just wish…." His voice trailed off and he didn't finish what he had started to say. He finally rose and headed for the room he was using, needing some time alone.

Chapter 18

Two days later, the two vehicles were headed back to town, relief in everyone's demeanour. Samuel turned his head to study Aideen. She had been quieter than usual for the last couple of days, working away with him, but not saying a lot, spending time alone. He sighed to himself, not quite sure what that meant. He just knew he didn't want to lose her, he wanted her a permanent part of his life. What they had been through put a constraint on him, though, he felt. He needed to give her time to get over this before he could approach her with his feelings.

Aideen knew Samuel was watching her. She didn't know quite what to do with him. They would have to talk soon, she knew, but for now her emotions were just too raw and open for her to even begin to make sense of what she was feeling. She needed her mother but didn't have her, not any more. She searched her mind for who she could talk to and finally decided she would talk to Phoebe when she could.

The vehicle doors swung open in Barnabas' driveway. Aideen hesitated for a moment before she stepped out, not sure she should be even here. Samuel reached for her hand and led her up to the door.

"It's okay, Aideen. You'll welcome to stay here for now. Dad wants that."

She nodded, her eyes searching for Barnabas. He wasn't there, nor was Timothy or Naomi. She sighed. Her questions and thanks would have to wait.

Sudden squealing of tires brought their heads around. Sudden popping of gunfire had them hitting the ground. Stephen and Silver returned fire, but the car was gone before they could hit anything. Richard pulled himself up to a sitting position, his hand on his arm where a bullet had sliced through his shirt sleeve. He turned as Stephen and Silver ran his way.

"Where'd they come from?" His voice was harsh.

"I have no idea. I've called it in. Only got a partial plate." Stephen's voice died away. "Samuel? Aideen?"

Richard turned, then stood, rushing over to where the couple lay crumpled.

Stephen reached for Samuel. "He's alive. Looks like it just grazed his head. Silver, help me. I need to move him off Aideen."

Gently they slid Samuel over onto his back. Richard reached with a cloth to try and stem the flow of blood from the head wound as he watched Stephen reach for Aideen. He could hear Silver called for paramedics.

"Stephen?" Richard's voice had the question he couldn't express.

"She's alive, Richard, but the bullet hit her in the back. I don't want to move her until we have help." He spun to stare at his team leader. "It's close to the spine."

Richard's eyes slid shut at the thought even as he heard the sirens approaching. He stood back and watched as the paramedics worked on both Samuel and Aideen. He shrugged off their help, pointing instead to the couple. He turned as they wheeled Samuel's stretcher away, nodding for Stephen to go with him. His phone chimed, and he pulled it out. Timothy was on the line.

"Richard? What's going on? We can't get down the street."

"No, we were ambushed, Timothy. Take Barnabas to the hospital. Let him know Samuel's been hurt and is on his way there."

"Samuel? How bad?"

"His head was grazed with a bullet."

"Aideen?"

Richard was silent and he could hear Timothy draw in a breath to speak.

"She's alive, Timothy. They're working on her now to transport."

"Where?"

"The back." He turned as Silver approached him. "Listen, they're ready to transport. I need to run. I'll meet you there."

Silver pointed to his arm. "You're riding with her. I'll stay here and see what I can come up with."

Richard nodded as he watched them load Aideen's stretcher into the rig before he headed that way himself. "Find out what you can. I want to know how they knew and who it was."

❧❧❧

Barnabas paced the waiting room on the surgical floor once more. Was it only a few weeks ago he had been here with Samuel? He turned as Richard approached, his sleeve torn off and a bandage around his arm.

"How's the arm?"

Richard took a look at it. "It's fine. Didn't even need stitches. I'm sorry, Barnabas. I should have known they'd try something."

Barnabas shook his head. "We all should have. We thought we had everyone. Andrew's officers are working through this. They don't like being shown up like this."

Richard gave a half-smile, then sobered. "Any word on Samuel yet?"

235

Samuel's father nodded, relief evident. "There's no fracture or brain bleeding. It just knocked him out. I've been in to see him. He's still unconscious but they think he'll be awake soon."

Richard nodded, then pointed at the chairs. "Let's sit. It's been a long day already."

Barnabas sank down, then looked up as footsteps approached. Silas stood watching them, then sank into a chair across from them.

"Silas. You're here."

"Where else would I be, Barnabas? You're my family. I need to be here with you. Faith has the prayer line working."

Barnabas nodded. "Thank her for me, will you? She and Josiah went through so much themselves."

Three hours later, Barnabas once more heard footsteps approaching and looked up. The surgeon stood in the doorway, still in his scrubs, mask down around his neck, surgical cap still on. The surgeon approached, waving Barnabas back to his seat, before he sank into a chair himself, fatigue evident as he pulled the cap off his head. He didn't speak, just sat.

"Joe?" Barnabas' friend was the surgeon and he was almost afraid to ask.

"Barnabas. The church must have been praying."

Barnabas nodded. "They were. Josiah's Faith got the prayer chain working."

"I could feel it in there, Barnabas. That young lady shouldn't be alive."

"It's that bad." Richard spoke, his eyes on Barnabas.

"It was. Right now, she's in recovery. We'll be moving her to ICU soon."

"Her injuries? She has no next of kin other than Samuel and me."

Joe nodded. "I know. That has to hurt, you know. Now, for her injuries, Stephen was right. It was near the spine, but didn't hit it. That area is quite swollen, which means it's interfering with the nerves to her legs. We're hoping that when the swelling goes down, movement comes back. We had to resect a kidney, the bullet penetrated it. It also clipped the bowel. If she hadn't had such quick aid, she wouldn't be in the shape she is."

Barnabas sat back, the implications and danger she was still in sinking in. "She's got a long road ahead of her, doesn't she?"

Joe nodded, his eyes sliding closed for a moment. "She does, Barnabas. She's in critical condition right now. Let us get her into a room and then I'll come find you." He looked at Richard. "I understand from your team that she's still under your protection. That's fine. We'll work around that. I don't want anything else to happen to her."

Richard spoke, his mind working to decide the best way to handle this. "We need a list of those who have access to her room. I want to vet them, and approve anyone who's going to be in there for any reason."

Joe nodded again. "I'll have the charge nurse get that information for you." He rose, hesitated as if to speak, then walked away.

Barnabas stood, his mind racing at what he had been told. Walking away from

Richard, he headed towards his son's room, praying for both the young people.

Samuel stirred as he awakened, his eyes adjusting to the dimness of the room, and groaned. Not again. Not the hospital again. His hand found the bandage on his head and he winced at the pain that shot through his head as it touched it.

"Son?" Barnabas stood by his son's bedside once more.

"Dad? What happened?"

"You were ambushed in the driveway at home. Your head was grazed with a bullet."

Samuel nodded, then regretted it. "I want out of here, Dad."

Barnabas gave a small laugh. "I know you do, but you're here overnight at least."

Samuel's eyes closed before he could say another word. Barnabas reached to pull the blankets up on his son, remembering the days when Samuel was young as he did so. He turned as he heard the door swish open.

"Barnabas?" Bill stood there.

"He's been awake, Bill. Not for very long, though."

Bill nodded. "Did he say anything?"

"Not really, other than saying he wants to leave." Barnabas turned to stare at Bill. "Where's the investigation stand?"

Bill shook his head. "We found the car, abandoned and reported as stolen. We're searching for the O'Dell boys. They've gone into hiding."

Barnabas thought about that. "It would be them, of course. They've always been on the wrong side of the law, haven't they? Find them, Bill. I won't rest until I know who did this to these two."

"None of us will. Andrew said he'd be by in a while. He's running something down, he said, some tidbit of information that he happened on."

"Happened on, did he? Where are the others on Richard's team?"

"Silver's with Aideen. Timothy is right outside this door along with one of our officers. Stephen's waiting in ICU for them to transfer Aideen to a bed there. Richard? He's with Andrew, wherever that is."

Barnabas nodded. "Thank you, Bill, for all your work. I didn't think it was over when we were sent home."

"No, it wasn't, but I don't think we expected a hit in the middle of the morning. They have had to have someone watching your place."

"I can guarantee they did. Check the house across the street. I have the key here. The people are away and I've been looking after it for them." He handed Bill the key, then froze. "That's where they'll be, Bill. Who would think of them being in a house in the neighbourhood where they just staged an attack?"

Bill nodded as he spun to leave. "Keep me updated. I'll be back as soon as I can." He almost ran from the room, phone to his ear.

Barnabas watched him walk away, then sank into the chair he had pulled up beside the bed. His head went back, and he slept, not hearing the movement around him as the nurses came and checked on Samuel. One found a blanket and gently covered him before heading back out of the room. He finally roused as a hand touched his shoulder.

Blinking, he looked up at Joe.

"Joe? Sorry, I didn't mean to fall alseep."

"You needed it, my friend. Come with me. We have Aideen in ICU. You can go see her for a while."

Barnabas hesitated, looking over at his son before he followed his friend down the hall to the ICU unit. He walked through the ICU unit doors, his heart lifted in prayer. Joe hadn't said how Aideen was yet.

Joe pointed to a cubicle. "We have her in this one, close to the unit desk, where the nurses can keep a good eye on her."

Barnabas stood and watched her for a moment. "How is she, really, Joe?"

"Really? Alive, thank God for that. Other than that, she's critical, Barnabas. We discussed what we had to do. I've put you and Samuel on her chart as next of kin, but that's just so we can talk to one another."

Barnabas nodded. "Any word on the swelling around her spine?"

"It's too early yet for anything to have changed." Joe sighed. "I pray it improves but it may not. Be prepared for that."

Barnabas sighed. "Who can prepare her for that? I don't know if her faith is strong enough to handle this." He stood, his eyes on the woman he had begun to think of as a daughter. His heart prayed, he couldn't say any words.

He finally turned, making his way back to his son. Why, Lord? Why did this happen?

Andrew found him finally, seated beside Samuel, his eyes on his sleeping son.

"Barnabas?"

Turning to study Andrew, Barnabas sighed. "I take it you don't have good news."

Andrew shook his head. "I don't. Those two men have disappeared. We looked in the house across from you but it looks as if they were never there."

Barnabas nodded. "It was a long shot, now wasn't it? Find the men who did this, Andrew. Find them before I do."

Andrew nodded, knowing that Barnabas would have called in his friends to search.

He spoke to Barnabas for a while longer before he left. He turned at the door, watching his friends, then sighing he walked away.

Chapter 19

$\mathcal{F}$our weeks later, Aideen took tentative steps around Barnabas' home, pushing her walker in front of her. She was glad to be out of the hospital, but unsure about being where she was. She knew just how close she had come to death, not waiting to be there ever again.

Samuel stood and watched, his heart in his eyes. He knew she wasn't ready to hear what he wanted to say. That was fine, it could wait. What he wanted to know was that they had found everyone, and he wasn't sure that they had. Andrew was still working on some information. Their assailants were still at large, not a comforting thought.

"Aideen, can I get you anything?" Samuel walked towards her as she sat on the couch.

She shook her head. "No, I'm fine, Samuel. You need to stop hovering."

He grinned. "Is that what I'm doing, hovering?"

She scowled at him. "That's exactly what you're doing. I know you have work to do and you can't do it if you're sitting here with me."

"Actually, I can. I have the programs on my laptop, the files I need with me, and a wireless connection to Dad's printer."

She shook her head again. "You need to go to your office and work."

"Not happening. There is no way we're leaving you here by yourself." He grinned as she scowled at him again. "Tough. Get used to it."

She sighed. "I'm sorry. It's just been a rough few months." She turned to stare at him. "Do you think we would have ever met if your Dad hadn't sent me here?"

Samuel shrugged. "I would like to think we would. Don't you think so?"

She studied him for a moment. "I doubt it very much, and I would hate not to have your friendship."

He sighed to himself, thinking that was how she saw him only, as a friend.

"I would like to think that somehow we would have. Regardless, God put us here, together, at this point in time." He reached to touch her shoulder. "I hate what you've gone through."

She stared at her hands, clasped together on her knees. "If I hadn't, I wouldn't have made the friends I have. I also wouldn't have found God in the way that I did. I wouldn't trade that, Samuel."

She stared at the door as the doorbell rang. "Were you expecting anyone?"

Samuel shook his head. "No, I wasn't, unless it's someone coming to check on you. Dad's said there's been a regular parade through here since you got home." He smirked at her as he rose and headed for the door.

Samuel's hand froze on the door as he saw the weapon pointed at him, and then raised his eyes to face the man, or rather men, in front of him. He was shoved backwards, barely keeping on his feet.

Aideen paled, seeing Samuel shoved backwards. She tried to rise, but the younger of the men was in front of her, pushing away her walker, and pinning her to her seat with a hand. Samuel tried to reach her, but was once more shoved back.

"You're a hard lady to find by yourself. And don't think the boyfriend here will keep you safe." The older man snarled at her. "We have orders to take you with us."

Aideen shook her head. "No, I'm not going anywhere with you."

Samuel pushed back against the man, sending him staggered away. The younger man swung at him, and Samuel ducked before slamming his body into him and sending them both to the floor. Aideen screamed as the two men fought for the weapon, neither gaining an inch. The older man fumbled for his, freezing as he felt metal against his neck.

"Give me one reason too." Richard snarled in his ear as he reached for the man's gun. "Hands on your head." He reached into his pocket for handcuffs, the click of their fastening a satisfying one. He then strode towards Samuel.

Samuel sat back, his breathing laboured as he stared down the man on the floor. He heard steps behind him and then a pair of handcuffs dangled in front of his face.

"I'll let you do the honours on this one." Richard's voice had a touch of amusement. "I just can't leave you two on your own, now can I?"

Samuel nodded his thanks as he tried to catch his breath, snapping the handcuffs on the man.

"How'd you manage to get here?" He took the hand Richard offered to pull him to his feet.

"I was just planning on stopping by to see how you two were doing, but it looks as if you two had everything under control."

"Not quite." Aideen had finally found her voice. "Thank you, once again, Richard. I gather you've called for Andrew or Bill?"

"I did when I saw the car in front of the house. It's one they've been looking for. I think you can finally say it's over. These two were the last of the bunch they were looking for." He looked around. "I would say that once Andrew and Bill have processed these two, they'll be by to update you on the case."

"And we want you and your team here. Please tell me you will be." Aideen's eyes sparkled with unshed tears.

Richard reached to hug her. "I wouldn't miss that for the world, nor would my team."

ക്കക്ക

A week later, Samuel studied everyone who had crowded into his father's living room. They really should move outside but the rain that had threatened that morning had moved in. He searched for Aideen, finding her with Silver and Naomi, Phoebe standing nearby. He turned as he felt a hand on his shoulder.

Andrew stood beside him, his eyes watchful.

"How are you now, Samuel?"

"I'm relieved it's finally over. I've had enough of this to last me a lifetime."

"You and Aideen both. Your dad as well, I suspect."

"I suspect he does. So, now that we're all here, are you going to spill the beans about what happened?"

Andrew laughed. "I'll do just that. Just wait a minute, though." He hesitated as if to say something and then shook his head.

"What?"

Andrew smirked. "I'll let you figure that out on your own, buddy. Hey, everyone, if I could have your attention, let me recap what the investigation showed."

Andrew approached Aideen, his face worried.

"Are you sure you're up for this?"

"I am. I want to know why." Aideen searched his face, her eyes then searching for Samuel.

"Okay, then." Andrew stood back, his eyes on the floor. "The story goes back fifty years, to a feud within a family. The O'Dells and O'Rourkes were cousins. One branch of the O'Rourke got involved in crime, namely that of buying off building inspectors and falsifying documents for clients. We've discovered there are a number of buildings here in town that really aren't safe. We've worked with the town engineer and are in the process of clearing out the buildings until they can be inspected and the inspections certified.

"Now, the O'Dells. They wanted in on the lucrative business, but the O'Rourkes wouldn't have any part of it. The O'Dells finally set up their own business of falsifying building titles to cover their other businesses of fraud and blackmail. Don't ask how that got done, we're still working on that.

"However, now to you, Aideen. Your family in no way was involved in this dirty business. Your Dad was a pastor, serving in a church outside of town. I didn't know that until a couple of days ago. You had been left with a family friend while they were on a trip to a conference for a day and were in a car accident. The friend decided they didn't want you and dumped you into foster care before any of your parents' families could speak up. You have a few people wanting to meet you. That's the good news for you.

"Now, as to how this all came about, your running to Barnabas and ending up here for your adventure we shall call it.

"Your boss is related to the O'Rourkes here in town. He knew of your connection and used it to his advantage. We believe he was the one who watched you all those years and set up the dummy temp service. You knew nothing about your history, so wouldn't have caught on to what he was doing. He was deeply involved in money laundering, falsifying building inspection reports, just to name a couple of crimes he would have been charge with. The men you heard that night were there to kill him, just as you suspected."

Andrew paused, his gaze running over everyone present. "Finally, it was the O'Dells who kidnapped you every time, just for spite twice. They were trying to send a message to the O'Rourkes that they wouldn't be messed with. I think that about wraps it up."

Conversation and speculation abounded as they filled plates and ate of the food that had been provided, finally breaking up to head home late that night.

Samuel hesitated as he watched Aideen move towards her bedroom, then turned. Tonight was not the night to talk to her. Soon, he would have to.

Barnabas watched as Samuel moved slowly towards his old room and nodded. Now that things were over, he thought, they would figure out they were meant to be. His eyes raised, he prayed for them both and for all that had just been there.

Epilogue

Samuel approached Aideen as she sat at the picnic table in his backyard a couple of weeks later. She had healed enough to be able to come back to work and had ditched the walker, as she put it. He sat beside her, his eyes studying her face.

"Aideen? Are you okay?" His voice was quiet.

"I finally think I am, Samuel." She turned to face him. "After all we went through, I finally get it that God was there all along, every step of the way. He used this to reach out to me, to teach me to trust Him when I had nothing else to trust in."

Samuel nodded. "He does that, Aideen. He'll use circumstances to reach us." He paused. "Do you have any regrets about your family?"

"I wish someone had taken me in as a baby, but they didn't get that chance. I get to know them now though, which in a way helps. I get to learn about my parents." She sighed. "I guess now I have to decide what I want to do and if I want to move to another town."

Samuel stared past her for a moment, not quite sure how to proceed or even if he should. "I hope you don't move away, Aideen."

She looked back at him, her eyes puzzled as she searched his face.

He brought his eyes down to watch her. "I would miss you if you left town. Not as a secretary. You've come to mean a lot to me." He stopped speaking, his eyes on his hands. "I guess what I'm saying is that I love you and would really like it if you stayed in town."

Aideen didn't speak, in fact couldn't. Tears sparkled in her eyes.

Samuel looked up, dismayed at the tears. "There, I've done it. I've made you cry. I'm sorry, Aideen. I shouldn't have said anything." He went to stand when her hand came down on his arm.

"Don't leave, Samuel. You took me by surprise, that's all. I never dreamed you felt like that." She watched as he nodded. "I won't leave town. I was going as I didn't think I could stay and see you all the time. You see, I love you too and have for weeks. I told you that in the letter I left you."

"You do? You really do? And I know you did." At her nod, he reached to sweep her into his arms. "Oh, Aideen, love, I've been waiting for you all my life." He raised his head to study her face and then lowered his to hers, capturing her lips in a kiss.

"Your Dad won't be surprised, you know." Aideen's laugh joined with his.

"No, I don't think he will be. God has blessed us, you know. Dad always wanted a daughter, and has hinted you'd make a good one."

"And I've always wanted a father. Your Dad is already that for me."

They sat, the sunset bathing them in a rosy glow, plans flowing from their mouths so quickly they couldn't stop. Barnabas stood on the deck, a smile on his face as he nodded and then looked up.

"I'd be thanking you, Lord, for keeping them safe and bring them together. They need one another, two half of a whole."   He wished Anna was here with him, but he somehow suspected that she knew.

Dear Readers

Thank you for taking the time to read through Samuel and Aideen's story. Life can suck sometimes, big time, but with faith in God, we're able to get through even the most difficult of days. He never fails us.

Once again, just as in *The Sparrow*, the first few paragraphs are an actual dream I had. Yeah, I know. I have weird dreams, the stuff books and movies are made of.

The knives Aideen suggested? Back when my parents had an old farmhouse (during the 1960s), they would use a knife in the basement door just as secondary lock. With it in place, it was hard to open the door. The windows she told Stephen how to remove? They are similar to ones I used to have to remove to clean. Bits and pieces of my experiences will show up in my books.

Now for the dirt bike. The idea for it came from a family member. I have a great-nephew, Rodrick Scott, who participates in flat track racing here in Ontario, Canada, with the aid of his father, Rod Scott, and their Triple-R Racing Team.

It is always a challenge to present a story that may sound the same as another but isn't really the same. I pray that the lessons Aideen and Samuel both learned speak to your heart.

The verses I chose were my Mom's. She would have them in every card she gave, every book she gave. She was the only one who knew that I had a dream to write a novel. *The Sparrow* was that book. Never be afraid of your dreams. God gives them to us. And He can and will provide a way for us to realize them.

Thank you once more.

Blessings.

Ronna